Herman Charles Bosman

RAMOUTSA ROAD

Compiled, with an
introduction and notes, by
Valerie Rosenberg

AD. DONKER/PUBLISHER

AD. DONKER (PTY) LTD
A Subsidiary of Donker Holdings (Pty) Ltd
P O Box 41021
Craighall
2024

First published 1987

ISBN 0 86852 130 2

Typeset by M.M. Fourie, Johannesburg
Printed and bound by Printpak Books,
Dacres Avenue, Epping

Contents

Acknowledgements

In compiling *Ramoutsa Road and Other Re-collected Stories* I thank Helena Lake, Herman Charles Bosman's widow and copyright-holder for her encouragement.

Lionel Abrahams, Bosman's pupil, unofficial literary executor, and friend gave unstintingly of his time and constructive criticism in selecting from *Almost Forgotten Stories* (first published by Howard Timmins in 1979) the pieces he believed should be retained in this volume, and in rereading some of the unpublished *Voorkamer* stories he agreed should be included. I acknowledge his contribution with a sense of privilege.

Human & Rousseau, publishers of my biography of Herman Charles Bosman, *Sunflower to the Sun*, gave permission to quote the introductory note to the *Voorkamer* pieces from it.

Valerie Rosenberg

Introduction

While researching the life of Herman Charles Bosman, I greatly enjoyed reading a number of short stories which were not previously available. Many of them had been published in long-forgotten periodicals of the 1930s; other, later, pieces had been excluded from the more recent collections.

These stories – some here collected for the first time – span over twenty years of Bosman's adult writing career. There are Oom Schalk Lourens stories, some veld stories, one prison story and some 'In die Voorkamer' pieces (first published in the now-defunct *The Forum*).

Bosman observed the socio-political scene, holding a mirror to life in stories that relate not just to the microcosm under scrutiny, but the human condition with all its idosyncracies. And like radar, they scan the humour threshold of his readers zeroing in on the appropriate level.

When I began to research his life story, I was asked by the Humanities Research Center at Austin, Texas (where the Bosman papers are lodged) whether I intended to do a data biography or an interpretative work. The short answer was 'a bit of both'. For early on I could see that Bosman drew no distinction between how an artist lived and what he created. The one was an extension of the other, and his advice on the matter was quite straightforward: 'If you have any poetry inside you, go into the world and live it. The verses will write themselves.'

All those pink and blue request slips for periodicals from the Johannesburg Public Library which I had filled in during the 1970s, provided a double dividend. There was the exciting encounter with 'new' stories: and then there was the tantalising task of matching them to the events in Bosman's life.

For three years I had the adventure of trailing the clues in a paperchase of contradictory information through Bosman's self-constructed smoke-screen. Actually, I should have considered myself warned.

In his story 'The Kafir Drum' (in *Unto Dust*), Bosman had his Black drum man suspect the efficacy of the new White telegraph operator because, not only is it important to have the right kind of person to send and receive news, but also to have the right person to recount it to.

This notion was more central to Bosman's thinking than most people realise. He is known to have told several different versions of the same story to different people varying it according to the person(s) addressed – or simply to suit his own mood.

But then, as his pupil, Lionel Abrahams put it:

> Regarding history, Herman Charles Bosman put the 'poet's embroidered lie' above the carefully authenticated factual account. He was not only more willing to hear the first than the second, but readier to believe it.

I consider this to be one of the most telling statements about Bosman and structured his biography *Sunflower to the Sun* around this theme.

In *Spotlight* magazine, along with the last Schalk Lourens story to appear during his lifetime, Bosman wrote a typical autobiographical note:

> I was born in Kuils River about fifteen miles from Cape Town, on February 3, 1905. A few years ago I revisited my birthplace. But there were no landmarks that I recognised. Nobody there had heard of me either.
>
> The most important educational influences in my life have been Jeppe High School, Witwatersrand University and unpropitious circumstances, the latter still acting as my mentor.
>
> After I had qualified as a schoolteacher the Transvaal Education Department, apparently with the intention of doing me a disservice, appointed me to a bushveld school in the Groot Marico. The disservice was to the Bushveld school. But while I was no good as a teacher I found in the

Marico a pattern of life offering infinite riches in literary material.

From schoolteaching I turned to journalism. It took me ten years on Fleet Street to learn that I wasn't any good at that either. I should have learned quicker . . .

Whilst I shall always regret my lack of direct exposure to Bosman's 'embroidered lie', it did prompt my curiosity to enquire objectively into some of these 'unpropitious circumstances' which so influenced his life.

At the age of twenty Herman Bosman acquired a teaching diploma and a wife, in that order. On Friday 21 February 1926, he borrowed £5 from Vera Sawyer, a young insurance clerk, gave his age as twenty-six, and married her under the name of Herbert Charles Boswell, leaving for his teaching post in the Marico the following Sunday without having consummated the marriage.

He returned for the July holidays with a hunting rifle, the weapon with which – in a moment of diminished responsibility – he mortally wounded his step-brother David Russell. He was given the death sentence, later commuted to eight years with hard labour, of which he eventually served three years and nine months at Pretoria Central Prison.

No responsible summary of the life of Herman Charles Bosman would be complete without reference to Ellie Beemer, the young Jewess, incarnated in his slim volume of erotica *The Blue Princess* just as no account could ignore his second wife Ellaleen Manson, who inspired the lines:

I sing of the morning I who have seen
Only the afternoons.
My westering heart is sunset stained,
But white where the langorous lips had been
Of Ellaleen.

Their relationship plunged down a path of destruction which was to leave him creatively impotent.

Bosman, quite correctly, did not think his *Spotlight* summary an appropriate place to mention the women in his life – even those who featured in its more propitious circumstances. Certainly not Helena, who gave him back his words, and certainly not his 'veld maiden' – that phantom love he pursued, in one or other guise, for all of his literary life.

Like Mark Twain, Bosman could never resist a good story about himself, even if he had to make it up. And so one discovers that the ten years he claimed to have spent as a Fleet Street journalist were actually only six. (He was in London from 1934 to 1940). As to that successful publishing venture of which he often spoke, the Arden Godbold Press, nowhere in the archives documenting press statistics in the United Kingdom for this period could I find any trace of it. He did, however, reside at what was supposed to be the address of the Press, but at the outbreak of World War II he vacated the premises abruptly without paying the rent. His effects which were sold for £1.10s.

Much later, the gentle Helena Stegmann, who became his third wife, and with whom he spent his last and most productive years, was his bewildered but uncomplaining accomplice in the elaborate lengths to which he went, straining an already ailing budget to the limit to convince the Receiver of Revenue that he was really a most successful author, who ought to be assessed in a higher tax bracket.

'The poet's embroidered lie' illumined Bosman's life with an essential truth far more potent than any apparent one. The apparent truth, after all, is relevant only as a frame of reference, which is the reason why this selection of stories, as far as possible, relates to chronological events in his life.

But facts are not to be worshipped. Just treated with respect. And not too much of that, either.

According to Bosman, unless an experience was perceived with trueness of vision, it could never be anything more than a fact recounted – no matter how authentic. But if it were truly *imagined*, then it could not fail to ring true – no matter how far-fetched.

If I were asked how much of Bosman's writing was true in the sense 'how much was based on personal experience?', then the answer would be 'a great deal'. But if the same question were phrased in respect of Bosman's highly individual *understanding* of the word 'truth', then the response should be '*All* of Bosman is true!'

Valerie Rosenberg

Notes for the stories are at the back of the book. The 'Voorkamer' pieces are grouped together in the text, and are the six which precede the title story 'Ramoutsa Road'.

On to Freedom

How we could tell that Gawie Prinsloo had been changed by his experiences on the diggings – Oom Schalk Lourens said – was when he came back from the diamond fields wearing a tie.

It was sad to see a young man altered so much by a few months of pick and shovel work on a claim. We came to the conclusion, however, that it wasn't the time he had spent on his claim with the pick and shovel that had changed Gawie Prinsloo: he must have got changed like that during those periods in which he didn't have a shovel in his hand, and the sweat wasn't dripping off him, and when he wasn't on his claim, even.

And judging by the way he had altered, it would seem that during much of Gawie Prinsloo's stay on the diggings he was not on the claim.

Of course, it was not a new thing in the bushveld for a young man to go to the diggings, fresh and unspoilt and God-fearing, and to come back different. Often at the Nagmaal the predikant would utter warnings about the dangers of the diamond fields; he would speak in solemn tones about what he called the false glitter of the alluvial diggings, and about the vanity of its carnal shows and sinful wordly riches. But it is just the unfortunate way of the world that many young men, who in the ordinary course would never have thought of leaving Marico, packed up and went to the diggings after they heard some of the things the predikant said about the wild sort of life that was led there, and about the evils of suddenly-acquired wealth.

The predikant was on occasion very outspoken in dealing with the shameful things that took place on the diggings, and it was noticeable that at such times certain members of his congregation would shuffle their feet and get restless at his language. And only afterwards the predikant would discover that the reason they were restless was because they wanted to be off to the diggings.

I can still remember a remark that Wynand Oosthuizen once made in regard to this matter. It was when we were preparing to leave Zeerust after the Nagmaal.

'As you all know,' Wynand Oosthuizen said, 'My farm is situated right up against the Limpopo, and I live there alone. Consequently, I have much time in which to think. And I have thought about this question of the predikant and the young men and the diamond diggings. Yes, I have given it much thought. And I perceive that there is only one way in which the predikant will be able to get people to stay away from the diamond fields: he must say that the diamond fields are a lot like heaven.'

We looked at Wynand Oosthuizen, wondering. It seemed to do queer things to a man, living alone like that beside the Limpopo.

Because we made no answer, Wynand Oosthuizen thought, apparently, that we hadn't understood what he was saying.

'You see,' he went on, 'after every Nagmaal I have observed that there is a big rush to the diamond diggings. That is because the predikant talks so much about the wickedness of life on the diggings; how the diamond fields are like Babylon, and how vice and evil flourish there, and how people make money there and then forget all about their duty to the church. Now, if the predikant were to say that the diggings are exactly like the Kingdom of Heaven, nobody would want to go. No, nobody at all.'

Wynand Oosthuizen winked, then, and set his hat at a slant and strode across to his ox-wagon. In silence, shaking our heads, we watched him getting ready to trek back to the Limpopo.

To do some more thinking, no doubt.

Then there was this matter of Gawie Prinsloo. As I have said, he was more changed than any other man that I had ever seen come back from the diggings. And I had seen many of them come back. Some came back with money that they didn't quite know what to do with: there seemed so much of it. Others came back penniless. One man whom I knew very well was reduced to selling his wagon and oxen on the diggings; and he returned to the Marico on foot, singing.

But Gawie Prinsloo was the only man who had ever come back from the diggings wearing a tie. What was more, it was a red tie; and Gawie Prinsloo said that he was wearing it for a political reason.

It was some time before I realised what Gawie Prinsloo meant by this. Then I proceeded to tell him about politics in the old days. Things were much better then, I said, and much simpler. Politics was concerned only with the question as to which man was going to be president.

'And if the wrong man got elected,' I said to Gawie, very pointedly, 'you merely inspanned and trekked out of the country. You didn't put on a red tie and walk about talking the sort of thing that you are talking now.'

Gawie thought that over for a little while. Then he said that it was cowardly to inspan and trek away from a difficulty. He explained that the right thing to do was to face a problem and to find a solution to it. It was easy to see, he said, how this spirit of trekking away had produced a race of men with weak characters and unenlightened minds.

Naturally, I asked him what he meant by a statement like that. I told him that in the past I had on several occasions trekked out of both the Transvaal and the Free State because I disapproved of the Presidents.

'Yes, Oom Schalk,' Gawie said, 'and look at you.'

From that remark, thoughtlessly uttered on a summer afternoon, you can see how much the diggings had altered Gawie Prinsloo.

Afterwards we found out that there were other points about Gawie's new politics besides the wearing of a red tie. For instance, he held views about kafirs that nobody in the Bushveld had ever heard of before. He spoke a great deal about freedom, and in between mentioning what a good thing freedom was he would mumble something to the effect that in the Marico the kafirs weren't being treated right.

But, of course, it was quite a while before we discovered the extent to which Gawie Prinsloo's mind had been influenced by this kind of politics. He introduced us to it gradually, as though he was afraid of the shock it might give us if he acquainted us with all his opinions right away.

One day, however, in the home of Jasper Steyn, the ouderling, a number of farmers questioned Gawie Prinsloo closely on his beliefs, and you can imagine the sensation that was caused when he admitted that, in his view, a kafir was just as good as a white man.

'Do you really mean to say,' Jasper Steyn, the ouderling, asked, choosing his words very carefully, 'that you can't see any important difference between a kafir and a white man?'

'No,' Gawie Prinsloo answered, 'There is only a difference of colour, and that doesn't count.'

Several of us burst out laughing at that; the ouderling rocked in his chair from side to side; you could hear him laughing right across in the next district, almost.

'Would you say,' the ouderling went on, wiping the tears out of his eyes, 'would you say that there is no difference between me and a kafir? Would you say, for instance, that I am just a white kafir?'

'Yes,' Gawie Prinsloo responded, promptly, 'but that's what I thought about you even before I went to the diggings.'

Subsequently, others took up the task of questioning Gawie Prinsloo. After he had got over his first sort of diffidence, however, there was no stopping him. He embarked on a long speech about justice and human rights and liberty; and what he kept on stressing all the time was what he called the wrongs of the kafirs.

It was easy to see that Gawie Prinsloo had been associating with a very questionable type of person on the diggings.

And because we knew that it was the diamond diggings that had led him astray we extended a great deal of tolerance towards his unusual utterances. We treated him as somebody who was not altogether responsible for what he said. In this way it became quite a fashionable pastime in the Marico for people to listen to Gawie Prinsloo talk. And he would talk by the hour about the way the kafirs were being oppressed.

'Look, Gawie,' I said to him once, 'why do you tell only the white people about the injustice that is being inflicted on the kafirs? Why don't you go and tell the kafirs about what is being done to them?'

Gawie told me that he had already done so.

'I have gone among the kafirs' he said, 'and I have told them about their wrongs.'

But he admitted that his talks didn't seem to do much good, somehow; because the kafirs just went on smoking dagga – inhaling it through water, he said.

'And when I have told them about their wrongs and about freedom they have laughed,' Gawie explained, looking very puzzled. 'Loudly.'

So the months passed, and Gawie Prinsloo's red tie got crinkled and faded-looking, and when Nagmaal came round again he was still in exactly the same position in regard to his politics; he still spoke fervently about justice for the kafirs, and he had not yet brought anybody round to his way of thinking. Moreover, he was no longer considered to be amusing. People began to remark that it was annoying to have to listen to his saying the same sort of thing over and over again; they also hinted that it was about time he left the bushveld.

It was then that Wynand Oosthuizen, once more coming to Zeerust for the Nagmaal, encountered Gawie Prinsloo and his faded red tie and his politics. Several of us were present at this meeting. By this time Gawie Prinsloo was slightly desperate with his message. He had grown so used to people not taking him seriously any more, that he had given up reasoning with them in a calm way. So it was in a markedly aggressive manner that he approached Wynand Oosthuizen.

'The kafirs?' Gawie Prinsloo called out to Wynand. 'The kafirs aren't getting justice in the Marico. And a kafir is just as good as you are.'

Gawie Prinsloo started to walk away, then: but Wynand Oosthuizen pulled him back – by his neck tie.

'Say that again,' Wynand demanded.

Nothing if not fearless, Gawie repeated what he had said, and a lot more besides.

Contrary to what we had expected, Wynand Oosthuizen did not get annoyed. Nor did he laugh. Instead, he pushed back his hat and looked intently at the young man with the washed-out red tie.

'This is something new,' he said slowly, 'I haven't heard that point of view before. And I can't tell whether you are right or wrong. But I have got an idea. My farm is in the far north, on the Limpopo, and I live there alone. I do a lot of thinking there. You come and stay with me until the next Nagmaal, and we will think this question out together.'

We were accustomed to Wynand Oosthuizen acting on occasion, in a singular fashion; it was well-known that the loneliness of his life by the Limpopo made his outlook different from that of most people. So we were not surprised at the nature of the invitation that he extended to Gawie Prinsloo. Nor were we surprised at Gawie Prinsloo's acceptance. For that matter, Gawie could not very well have done anything else: Wynand Oosthuizen was holding him so firmly by the tie.

'I will come with you,' Gawie Prinsloo said, 'but I know that I am right.'

Thus, it was that they met in Zeerust and arranged to travel together to the Limpopo, to study the new politics about freedom and about equal rights for the kafirs – Wynand Oosthuizen, the lonely thinker, and Gawie Prinsloo, the young firebrand.

They agreed to meet again in church; at the Nagmaal, and to trek away as soon as possible after the service was over.

And I often wondered, subsequently, to what extent it was the predikant's sermon that had influenced two men who had planned to sojourn by the Limpopo and think of freedom. Because, in the morning, after the Nagmaal service, when Wynand Oosthuizen trekked away in his ox-wagon, Gawie Prinsloo was with him, and together they travelled the long and dusty road that led south, away from the thorn-trees of the Low Veld, to the diggings.

The Night-dress

Johanna Snyman stood in front of the kitchen table on which lay a pile of washing. It was ordinary farm clothing; her father's and brothers' blue jean shirts and trousers, her mother's and her own dresses and underwear.

Johanna took an iron off the stove, tilted it sideways and spat on it to see if it was hot. Then she went back to the table and commenced ironing.

It was a hot day in the Marico Bushveld. The heat from the sun and from the stove made the kitchen unbearable for Johanna's mother, who had gone to sit in front of the house with some sewing and a back number of the *Kerkbode*. Johanna's mother was known all over the district as Tant Lettie. She was thin and sallow-looking and complained regularly about her health. There was something the matter with her which rooi laventel, wit dulsies and other Boer remedies could not cure.

On the other hand, Johanna was strong and robustly made. Now, with the heat of the kitchen there was a pink glow on her features. It was a flush that extended from her forehead right down to her neck and that part of her bosom which the blue print frock did not conceal. Her face was full and had just that tendency towards roundness that is much admired by the men of the bushveld. But her nose was too small and too snub to remain attractive long after girlhood. And Johanna was twenty-three.

Tant Lettie, having put aside the *Kerkbode*, began embroidering a piece of cheap material that she had bought from the Indian store at Ramoutsa. She was making herself a night-dress. She held the partly-finished garment to the light and examined it. She laughed softly. But it was not a meaningless laugh. There was too much bitterness in it for that. She wondered why she was taking all that trouble with her night-dress, sewing bits of pink tape on it and working French knots round the neck, for all the world as though she was making it for her honeymoon.

She remembered the time she got married. Twenty-four years ago. A long while beforehand she had made herself clothes. That was on the Highveld, in the Potchefstroom district. Her father had sold some oxen to the Jew trader and had given her the money to buy things for her marriage. That was a good time. She remembered that one night-dress she made. It was very fine stuff that cost one riks-daler a yard. She sewed on a lot of lace, and put in all kinds of tucks and frills. When it was finished it was pretty. She ironed it out and put it right at the bottom of the kist in her bedroom. She didn't want any of her brothers or sisters to see that night-dress, because they would make improper jokes about it and she would feel uncomfortable. As it was, they already had too much to say.

They went by Cape-cart to Potchefstroom for the wedding. Frans Snyman looked very happy. But he was excited and she was afraid he would drop the ring, and that would bring them bad luck. But he did not drop it, and yet they seemed to have got bad luck all the same. When the ceremony was over, Frans kissed her and said: 'Now you will always be my wife.' She felt afraid when he said that.

That night they stayed at her father's house. Then she and Frans left for the Government farm that Frans had bought in the Marico Bushveld. She remembered the way she had taken the night-dress out of the kist that evening after the wedding, and how she had laughed at the frills in it, and the ribbons and the lace, and had suddenly folded up the garment against her breasts. But that was long ago.

She had kept the night-dress for many years. Often she looked at it and thought of the time when she had first worn it. But, somehow, it didn't seem the same. Each time she took it out it meant less to her than before. Afterwards she made a petticoat out of it for Johanna.

First Johanna was born. Then came, in turn, Willem and Adrian and Lourens. In the first year of their marriage there was a big drought, and it was only after half the stock had died that Frans decided to trek with the remainder of the stock to the Limpopo River. It was in the ox-wagon that Johanna was born. Tant Lettie remembered that she was alone nearly all that day, with only a kafir woman to attend to her. And Frans was in a bad temper because the kafirs had been negligent and had allowed some oxen to get lost. Frans was also angry because she had not given birth to a man-child. He swore about it, as though it was her fault.

Later on, when Willem was born, Frans seemed a little more satisfied. But it was only for a while. There were other things that he had to concern himself with. It had rained and he had to sow mealies all day as long as the ground remained wet. As for the two youngest children, Adrian and Lourens, Frans hardly noticed their coming.

Still, that was the way Frans was, and all men were like that. She knew he was sorry he had got married, and she didn't blame him for it. Only she thought that he need not always show it in such an open sort of way. For that matter, she was sorry also that she had got married. It would have been better if she had remained in her father's house. She knew she would have been unhappy there, and when her parents died she would have to go out and stay with somebody else. Or she might have been able to get work somewhere. But still, all that would have been much better that to get married. Now she had brought four children into the world who would lead the same kind of life that she had led.

Tant Lettie put down her sewing. Her face turned slightly pale. Her hands dropped to her sides. She felt, coming on once more, that pain which rooi laventel and wit dulsies could not cure.

In the kitchen Johanna had at last finished with the washing. Then she slipped quietly into her bedroom and came back with a garment which she unfolded in a way that had tenderness in it. She ran her fingers over the new linen, with the lace and ribbons and frills. Then, having ironed it, she took the night-dress to her bedroom and packed it away carefully at the bottom of her kist.

Francina Malherbe

After her father's death, Oom Schalk Lourens said, Francina Malherbe was left alone on the farm Maroelasdal. We all wondered then what she would do. She was close on to thirty and in the bushveld, when a girl is not married by twenty-five, you can be quite certain that she won't get a man any more. Unless she has got money. And even then if she gets married at about thirty she is liable to be left afterward with neither money nor husband. Look at what happened to Grieta Steyn.

But with Francina Malherbe it was different.

I remember Francina as a child. She was young when Flip first trekked into the bushveld. There was an unlucky man for you. Just the year after he had settled on Maroelasdal the rinderpest broke out and killed off all his cattle. That was a bad time for all of us. But Flip Malherbe suffered most. Then, for the first time that anybody in the Marico District could remember, a pack of wolves came out of the Kalahari, driven into the Transvaal by the hunger. For in the Kalahari nearly all the game had died with the rinderpest. Maroelasdal was the nearest farm to the border, and in one night, as Flip told us, the wolves got into his kraal and tore the insides out of three hundred of his sheep. This was all the more remarkable, because Flip, to my knowledge, had never owned more than fifty sheep.

Then Flip Malherbe's wife died of the lung disease, and shortly afterwards also his two younger sons who were always delicate. That left only Francina, who was then about fifteen. All those troubles turned Flip's head a little. That year the Government voted money for the relief of farmers who had suffered from the rinderpest, and Flip put in a claim. He got paid quite a lot of money, but he spent most of it in Zeerust on drink. Then Flip went to the schoolteacher and asked him if the Government would not give him compensation also because his wife and his sons had died, but the teacher, who did not know that Flip had become strange in the head, only laughed at him. Often after that, Flip told us that he was sorry his wife and children had died of the lung disease instead of the rinderpest, because otherwise he could have put in a claim for them.

Francina left school and set to work looking after the farm. With what was left out of the money Flip had got from the Government, she bought a few head of cattle. When the rains came she bought seed mealies and set the kafir squatters ploughing the vlakte. For three months in the year, by law, the kafirs have to work for the White man on whose land they live. But you know what it is with kafirs. As soon as they saw that there was no man on the farm who would look to it that they worked, the kafirs ploughed only a little every day for Flip and spent the rest of the time in working for themselves. Francina spoke to her father about it, but it was no good. Flip just sat in front of the house all day smoking his pipe. In the end, Francina wrote out all the trekpasses and made all the kafirs clear off the farm, except old Mosigo, who had always been a good kafir.

In those days, Francina was very pretty. She had dark eyes with long lashes that curled down on her red cheeks when her eyes were closed. I know, because I usually sat near her in church, and during prayers I sometimes looked sideways at her. That was sinful, but then I was not the only one who did it. Whenever I opened my eyes slightly to look at her, I saw that there were other men doing the same thing. Once a young minister, who had just finished his studies at Potchefstroom, came to preach to us, so that we could appoint him as our predikant if we wished. But we did not appoint him. The ouderlings and diakens in the church council said that perhaps they could permit a minister to look underneath his lids while he was praying, but it was only right that his eyes be shut all the time when he pronounced the blessing.

For the next two years I don't know how Francina and her father managed to make a living on the farm. But they did it somehow. Also, after a while they got other kafir families to squat on the farm, and to help Mosigo on the lands with the ploughing time. Once Flip left his place on the front stoep and got into the mule-cart and drove to Zeerust. After two days, the hotel proprietor sent him back to the farm on an Indian trader's wagon. Flip had sold the mules and cart and bought drink.

Shortly after that I saw Flip at the post office. The dining-room of Hans Welman's house was the post office, and we all went there to talk and fetch our letters. Flip came in and shook hands with everybody in the way we all did, and said good morning. Then he went up to Hans Welman and held out his hand. Welman just looked Flip Malherbe up and down and walked away. But with all his nonsense, Flip was sane enough to know that he had been insulted.

'You go to hell, Hans Welman,' he shouted.

Welman turned round at once.

'My house is the public post office,' he said, 'so I can't throw you out. But I can say what I think of you. You treat your daughter like a kafir. You're a low, drunken mongrel.'

We could see that Flip Malherbe was afraid, but he could do nothing else after what the other man had said to him. So he went up to Welman and hit him on the chest. Welman just grabbed Flip quickly by the collar. Then he ran with him to the door, spun him round and kicked him under the jacket.

'Filth,' he said, when Flip fell in the dust.

We all felt that Hans Welman had no business to do that. After all, it was Flip's own affair as to how he treated his daughter.

After that we rarely saw Flip again. He hardly ever moved from his front stoep. At first young men still came to call on Francina. But later on they stopped coming, for she gave them no encouragement. She said she could not marry while her father was still alive as she had to look after him. That was usually enough for most young men. They had only to glance once at Flip, who of late had grown fat and hearty looking, to be satisfied that it would still be many years before they could hope to get Francina. Accordingly, the young men stayed away.

By and by nobody went to the Malherbe's house. It was no use calling on Flip, because we all knew he was mad. Although, often, when I thought of it, it seemed to me that he was less insane than people believed. After all, it is not every man who can so arrange his affairs that he has nothing more to do except to sit down all day smoking and drinking coffee.

But although Francina never visited anybody, she always went regularly to church. Only, as the years passed, she became thinner and there were wrinkles under her eyes. Also, her cheeks were no longer red. And there are always enough fresh-looking girls in the bushveld, without the young men having to trouble themselves overmuch about those who have grown old.

And so the years passed, as you read in the Book, summer and winter and seed-time and harvest. Then one day Flip Malherbe died. The only people at the funeral were the Bekkers, the Van Vuurens, my family and Hendrik Oberholzer, the ouderling who conducted the service. We saw Francina scatter dust over her father's face and then we left.

That was the time when we began to wonder what Francina would do. It was fifteen years since her mother had died, so that Francina was now thirty, and during those fifteen years she had worked hard and in a careful way, so that the farm Maroelasdal was all paid and there was plenty of sheep and cattle. But Francina just went on exactly the same as she had done when her father was still alive. Only, now the best years of a woman's life were behind her, and during all that time she had had nothing but work. We all felt sorry for her, the womenfolk as well, but there was nothing we could do.

Francina came to church every Sunday, and that was about the only time we saw her. Yet both before and after the church she was always alone, and she seldom spoke to anybody. In her black mourning dress she began to look almost pretty again, but of what use was that at her age?

People who had trekked into the Marico District in the last four years and only knew her by sight said she must also be a little strange in the head, like her father was. They said it looked as though it was in the family. But we who saw her grow up knew better. We understood that it was her life that had made her lonely like that.

One day an insurance agent came through the bushveld. He called at all the houses, Francina's also. It did not seem as if he was doing much business in the district, and yet every time he came back. And people noticed that it was always to Francina's house that the insurance agent went first. They talked about it.

But if Francina knew what was being said about her she never mentioned it to anybody, and she didn't try to act differently. Nevertheless, there came a Sunday when she missed going to church. At once everybody felt that what was being whispered about her was true. Especially when she did not come to church the next Sunday or the Sunday after. Of course, stories that are told in this way about women are always true. But there was one thing that they said that was a lie. They said that what the insurance agent wanted was Francina's farm and cattle. And they foretold that exactly the same thing would happen to Francina as had happened to Grieta Steyn: that in the end she would lose both her property and the man.

As I have told you, this last part of their stories did not come out in the way they had prophesied. If the insurance agent really had tried to get from her the farm and the cattle, nobody could say for sure. But what we did know was that he had gone back without them. He left quite suddenly, too, and he did not return any more.

And Francina never again came to church. Yes, it's funny that women could get like that. For I did not imagine that anything could ever come across Francina's life that would make her go away from her religion. But, of course, you can't tell.

Sometimes when I ride past Maroelasdal in the evening, on my way home, I wonder about these things. When I pass that point near the aardvark mound where the trees have been chopped down, and I see Francina in front of the house, I seem to remember her again as she was when she was fourteen. And if the sun is near to setting, and I see her playing with her child I sometimes wish somehow that it was not a bastard.

Karel Flysman

It was after the English had taken Pretoria that I first met Karel Flysman, Oom Schalk Lourens said.

Karel was about twenty-five. He was a very tall, well-built young man with a red face and curly hair. He was good-looking, and while I was satisfied with what the good Lord had done for me, yet I felt sometimes that if only He had given me a body like what Karel Flysman had got, I would go to church oftener and put more in the collection plate.

When the big commandos broke up, we separated into small companies, so that the English would not be able to catch all the Republican forces at the same time. If we were few and scattered the English would have to look harder to find us in the dongas and bushes and *rante*. And the English, at the beginning, moved slowly. When their scouts saw us making coffee under the trees by the side of the spruit, where it was cool and pleasant, they turned back to the main army and told their general about us. The general would look through his field-glasses and nod his head a few times.

'Yes,' he would say, 'that is the enemy. I can see them under those trees. There's that man with the long beard eating out of a pot with his hands. Why doesn't he use a knife and fork? I don't think he can be a gentleman. Bring out the maps and we'll attack them.'

Then the general and a few of his commandants would get together and work it all out.

'This cross I put here will be those trees,' the general would say. 'This crooked line I am drawing here is the spruit, and this circle will stand for the pot that that man is eating out of with his fingers. . . . No, that's no good, now. They've moved the pot. Wonderful how crafty these Boers are.'

Anyway, they would work out the plans of our position for half an hour, and at the end of that time they would find out that they had got it all wrong. Because they had been using a map of the Rustenburg District, and actually they were half-way into the Marico. So by the time they had everything ready to attack us, we had already moved off and were making coffee under some other trees.

How do I know all these things? Well, I went right through the Boer War, and I was only once caught. And that was when our commandant, Apie Terblanche, led us through the bushveld by following some maps that he had captured from the British. But Apie Terblanche never was much use. He couldn't even hang a Hottentot properly.

As I was saying, Karel Flysman first joined up with our commando when we were trekking through the bushveld north of the railway line from Mafeking to Barberton. It seemed that he had got separated from his commando and that he had been wandering about through the bush for some days before he came across us. He was mounted on a big black horse and, as he rode well, even for a Boer, he was certainly the finest-looking burgher I had seen for a long time.

One afternoon, when we had been in the saddle since before sunrise, and had also been riding hard the day before, we off-saddled at the foot of a koppie, where the bush was high and thick. We were very tired. A British column had come across us near the Malopo River. The meeting was a surprise for the British as well as for us. We fought for about an hour, but the fire was so heavy that we had to retreat, leaving behind us close on to a dozen men, including the veldkornet. Karel Flysman displayed great promptitude and decision. As soon as the first shot was fired he jumped off his horse and threw down his rifle; he crawled away from the enemy on his hands and knees. He crawled very quickly too. An hour later, when we had ourselves given up resisting the English, we came across him in some long grass about a mile away from where the fighting had been. He was still crawling.

Karel Flysman's horse had remained with the rest of the horses, and it was just by good luck that Karel was able to get into the saddle and take to flight with us before the English got too close. We were pursued for a considerable distance. It didn't seem as though we would ever be able to shake off the enemy. I suppose that the reason they followed us so well was because that column could not have been in charge of a general; their leader must have been only a *kaptein* or a commandant, who probably did not understand how to use a map.

It was towards the afternoon that we discovered that the English were no longer hanging on to our rear. When we dismounted in the thick bush at the foot of the koppie, it was all we could do to unsaddle our horses. Then we lay down on the grass and stretched out our limbs and turned round to get comfortable, but we were so fatigued that it was a long time before we could get into restful positions.

Even then we couldn't get to sleep. The commandant called us together and selected a number of burghers who were to form a committee to try Karel Flysman for running away. There wasn't much to be said about it. Karel Flysman was young, but at the same time he was old enough to know better. An ordinary burgher has got no right to run away from a fight at the head of the commando. It is the general's place to run away first. As a member of this committee I was at pains to point all this out to the prisoner.

We were seated in a circle on the grass. Karel Flysman stood in the centre. He was bare-headed. His Mauser and bandolier had been taken away from him. His trousers were muddy and broken at the knees from the way in which he had crawled that long distance through the grass. There was also mud on his face. But in spite of all that, there was a fine, manly look about him, and I am sure that others besides myself felt sorry that Karel Flysman should be so much of a coward.

We were sorry for him, in a way. We were also tired, so that we didn't feel like getting up and doing any more shooting. Accordingly we decided that if the commandant warned him about it we would give him one more chance.

'You have heard what your fellow-burghers have decided about you,' the commandant said. 'Let this be a lesson to you. A burgher of the Republic who runs away quickly may rise to be commandant. But a burgher of the Republic must also know that there is a time to fight. And it is better to be shot by the English than by your own people, even though,' the commandant added, 'the English can't shoot straight.'

So we gave Karel Flysman back his rifle and bandolier, and we went to sleep. We didn't even trouble to put out guards round the camp. It would not have been any use putting out pickets, for they would have been sure to fall asleep, and if the English did come during the night they would know of our whereabouts by falling over our pickets.

As it happened, that night the English came.

The first thing I knew about it was when a man put his foot on my face. He put it on heavily, too, and by the feel of it I could tell that his veldskoens were made of unusually hard ox-hide. In those days, through always being on the alert for the enemy, I was a light sleeper, and that man's boot on my face woke me up without any difficulty. In the darkness I swore at him and he cursed back at me, saying something about the English. So we carried on for a few moments: he spoke about the English; I spoke about my face.

Then I heard the commandant's voice, shouting out orders for us to stand at arms. I got my rifle and found my way to a sloot where our men were gathering for the fight. Up to that moment it had been too dark for me to distinguish anything that was more than a few feet away from me. But just then the clouds drifted away, and the moon shone down on us. It happened so quickly that for a brief while I was almost afraid. Everything that had been black before suddenly stood out pale and ghostly. The trees became silver with dark shadows in them, and it was amongst these shadows that we strove to see the English. Wherever a branch rustled in the wind or a twig moved, we thought we could see soldiers. Then somebody fired a shot. At once the firing became general.

I had been in many fights before, so that there was nothing new to me in the rattle of Mausers and Lee-Metfords, and in the red spurts of flame that suddenly broke out all round us. We could see little of the English. That meant that they could see even less of us. All we had to aim at were those spurts of flame. We realised quickly that it was only an advance party of the English that we had up against us. It was all rifle fire;

the artillery would be coming along behind the main body. What we had to do was to go on shooting a little longer and then slip away before the rest of the English came. Near me a man shouted that he was hit. Many more were hit that night.

I bent down to put another cartridge-clip into my magazine, when I noticed a man lying flat in the sloot, with his arms about his head. His gun lay on the grass in front of him. By his dress and the size of his body I knew it was Karel Flysman. I didn't know whether it was a bullet or cowardice that had brought him down in that way. Therefore, to find out, I trod on his face. He shouted out something about the English, whereupon (as he used the same words), I was satisfied that he was the man who had awakened me with his boot before the fight started. I put some more of my weight on to the foot that was on his face.

'Don't do that. Oh, don't,' Karel Flysman shouted. 'I am dying. Oh, I am sure I am dying. The English . . .'

I stooped down and examined him. He was unwounded. All that was wrong with him was his spirit.

'God,' I said; 'why can't you try to be a man, Karel? If you've got to be shot nothing can stop the bullet, whether you are afraid or whether you're not. To see the way you're lying down there anybody would think that you are at least the commandant-general.'

He blurted out a lot of things, but he spoke so rapidly and his lips trembled so much that I couldn't understand much of what he said. And I didn't want to understand him, either. I kicked him in the ribs and told him to take his rifle and fight, or I would shoot him as he lay. But of course all that was of no use. He was actually so afraid of the enemy that even if he knew for sure that I was going to shoot him he would just have lain down where he was and have waited for the bullet.

In the meantime the fire of the enemy had grown steadier, so that we knew that at any moment we could expect the order to retreat.

'In a few minutes you can get back to your old game of running,' I shouted to Karel Flysman, but I don't think he heard much of what I said, on account of the continuous rattle of the rifles.

But he must have heard the word 'running'.

'I can't,' he cried. 'My legs are too weak. I am dying.'

He went on like that some more. He also mentioned a girl's name. He repeated it several times. I think the name was Francina. He shouted out the name and cried out that he didn't want to die. Then a whistle blew, and shortly afterwards we got the order to prepare for the retreat.

I did my best to help Karel out of the sloot. The Englishmen would have laughed if they could have seen that struggle in the moonlight. But the affair didn't last too long. Karel suddenly collapsed back into the sloot and lay still. That time it was a bullet. Karel Flysman was dead.

Often after I have thought of Karel Flysman and of the way he died. I have also thought of that girl he spoke about. Perhaps she thinks of her lover as a hero who laid down his life for his country. And perhaps it is as well that she should think that.

Visitors to Platrand

When Koenrad Wium rode back to his farm at Platrand, in the evening, with fever in his body and blood on his face (Oom Schalk Lourens said), nobody could guess about the sombre thing that was in his heart.

It was easy to guess about the fever, though. For, that night, when he lay on his bed, and the moon shone in through the window, Lettie Wium, his sister, had to shut out the moonlight with a curtain, because of the way that Koenrad kept on trying to rise from the bed in order to blow out the moon.

Koenrad Wium had gone off with Frik Engelbrecht into the Protectorate. They took with them rolls of tobacco and strings of coloured beads, which they were going to barter with the kafirs for cattle.

When he packed his last box of coloured beads on the wagon, Koenrad Wium told me that he and Frik Engelbrecht expected to be away a long time. And I said I suppose they would. That was after I had seen some of the beads.

I knew, then, that Koenrad Wium and Frik Engelbrecht would have to go into the furthest parts of the Protectorate, where only the more ignorant kind of kafirs are.

Koenrad was very enthusiastic when they set out. But I could see that Frik Engelbrecht was less keen. Frik was courting Koenrad's sister, Lettie. And Lettie's looks were not of the sort that would make a man regard a box of beads as a good enough excuse for departing on a long journey out of the Marico.

I felt that his chief reason for going was that he wanted to oblige his future brother-in-law. And this was quite a strange reason.

'The only trouble,' Koenrad said, 'is that when I get back I'll have to go and live in a bigger district than the Marico. Otherwise I won't have enough space for all my cattle to move about in. The Dwarsbergen take up too much room.'

But Frik Engelbrecht did not laugh at Koenrad's joke. He only looked sullen.

And I remember what Lettie answered, when her brother asked her what she would like him to give her for a wedding present, when he had made all that money.

'I would like,' Lettie said, after thinking for a few moments, 'some beads.'

It was singular, therefore, that when Koenrad came back it was without the cattle. And without Frik Engelbrecht. And without the beads.

And he said strange things with the fever on him. He was sick for a long while. And with wasted cheeks, and a hollow look about his eyes, and his forehead bandaged with a white rag, Koenrad Wium lay in bed and talked mad words in his delirium. Consequently, on the days that the lorry from Zeerust came to the post office, there was not the usual crowd of bushveld farmers discussing the crops and politics. They did not come to the post office any more; they went, instead, to the farm house at Platrand, where they smoked and drank coffee in the bedroom and listened to Koenrad's babblings.

When the ouderling got to hear about these goings-on, he said it was very scandalous. He said it was a sad thing for the Dopper Church that some of its members could derive amusement from listening to the ravings of a delirious man. The ouderling had a keen sense of duty, and he was not content with merely reprimanding those of his neighbours whom he happened to meet casually. He went straight up to Koenrad's house in Platrand, right into the bedroom, where he found a lot of men sitting around the wall; they were smoking their pipes and occasionally winking at one another.

The ouderling remained there for several hours. He sat very stiffly on a chair near the bed. He glared a good deal at the farmers to show how much he despised them for being so low. And I noticed that the only time his arms were not folded tightly across his chest was when he had one hand up to his ear, owing to the habit that Koenrad had, sometimes, of mumbling. The ouderling was a bit deaf.

And all this time Lettie would pass in and out of the room, silently. She greeted us when we came, and brought us coffee, and said goodbye to us again when we left. But it was hard to gather just exactly what Lettie thought of the daily visits of ours. For she said little. Just those cool words when we left. And those words, when we came, that we noticed were cooler.

In fact, during the whole period of Koenrad's illness, she spoke on only one other occasion. That was on the third day the ouderling called. And it was to me that she spoke, then.

'I think, Oom Schalk, it is bad for my brother,' Lettie said, 'if you sit right on top of him, like that. If you can't hear too well what he is saying, you can bend your ear over with your hand, like the ouderling does.'

It was hard to follow the drift of Koenrad's remarks. For he kept on bringing in things that he did as a boy. He spoke very much about his childhood days. He told us quite instructive things, too. For instance, we never knew, until then, that Koenrad's father stole. Several times he spoke about his father, and each time he ended up by saying, in a thin sort of voice: 'No, father, you must not steal so much. It is not right.' He would also say: 'You may laugh, now father. But one day you will not laugh.'

It was on these occasions that we would look at one another and wink. Sometimes Lettie would come into the room while Koenrad was saying these things about their father. But you could not tell by her face that she heard. There was just that calm and distant look in her eyes.

But we listened most attentively when Koenrad spoke about his trek into the Protectorate with Frik Engelbrecht. He said awful things about thirst and sin and fever, and we held our breath in fear that we should miss a word. It gave me a queer sort of feeling, more than once, to be sitting in that room of sickness, looking at a man with wasted cheeks, whose cracked lips were mumbling dark words. And in the midst of these frightening things he would suddenly talk about little red flowers that lay on the grass. He spoke about the foot of a hill where shadows were. He spoke as though these flowers were the most dreadful part of the story.

It was always at this stage that the argument started amonst the men sitting in the room.

Piet Snyman said it was all nonsense, the first time that Koenrad mentioned the flowers. Piet said that he had never seen any red flowers in the Protectorate, and he had been there often.

Stephanus Naude agreed with him, and said that Koenrad was just trying to be funny with us, now, and was wasting our time. He said he didn't get up early every morning and ride sixteen miles to hear Koenrad Wium discuss flowers. Piet Snyman sympathised with Stephanus Naude, and said that he himself had almost as far to ride. 'While Koenrad tells us about himself and Engelbrecht, or about his father's dishonesty, we can listen to him,' Piet added.

The ouderling held up his hand.

'Broeders,' he said, 'let us not judge Koenrad Wium too harshly. Maybe he already had the fever, then, when he thought he saw the red flowers.'

Piet Snyman said that was all very well, but then why couldn't Koenrad tell us so straight out? 'After all, we are his guests.' Piet explained. 'We sit here and drink his coffee, and then he tries to be funny.'

There was much that was reasonable in what Piet Snyman said.

We said that Koenrad was not being honest with us, and that it looked as though he had inherited that dishonesty from his father. We said, further, that he wasn't grateful for the trouble we were taking over him. He seemed to forget that it didn't happen to just any sick person to have half the able-bodied men in the Marico watching at his bedside. Practically day and night, you could say. And sitting as near the bed as Lettie would allow us.

Gradually Koenrad began to get better.

But before that happened a kafir brought a message to us from the man in charge of the Drogevlei post office. The man wanted to know if we would like to have our letters re-addressed to Koenrad Wium's house at Platrand. We realised that it was a sarcastic message, and when we had pointed this out to the ouderling, he went to the back of the house and kicked the kafir for bringing it.

Koenrad's recovery was slow. But when he regained consciousness he did not talk much. Furthermore, he seemed to have no recollection of the things he had said in his days of delirium. He seemed to remember nothing of his mumblings about his boyhood, and about Engelbrecht and the Bechuanaland Protectorate. And although the ouderling questioned him, subtly, when Lettie was in the kitchen and the bedroom door was closed, there was not much that we could learn from his replies.

'Take your father, for instance,' the ouderling said – and we looked significantly at one another – 'Can you remember him in the old days, when you were living in the Cape?'

'Yes,' Koenrad answered.

'And did they ever – I mean,' the ouderling corrected himself. 'Did your father ever go away from the house for, say, six months?'

'No,' Koenrad replied.

'Twelve months, then?'

'No,' Koenrad replied.

'Did you ever see him walking about?' the ouderling asked. 'With a red handkerchief over the lower part of his face?' We could see from this question, that the ouderling had more exciting ideas than we had about the sort of things that a thief does.

'No,' Koenrad said again, looking surprised.

All Koenrad's replies were like that – unsatisfactory. Still, it wasn't the ouderling's fault. We knew that the ouderling had done his best. Piet Snyman's methods, however, were not the same as the ouderling's. His words were not so well thought out.

'You don't seem to remember much about your father – huh?' Piet Snyman said. 'But what about all those small red flowers lying around on the grass?'

The change that came over Koenrad Wium's face at this question was astonishing. But he didn't answer. Instead, he drew the blanket over his head and lay very still. Piet Snyman was still trying to pull the blanket off his face again, when Lettie walked into the bedroom.

'Your brother has had a relapse,' the ouderling said to

Lettie.

Lettie looked at the ouderling without speaking. She picked up the quinine bottle and knelt at Koenrad's bedside.

Koenrad relapsed quite often after that, when Lettie was in the kitchen. He relapsed four time over questions that the ouderling asked him, and seven times over things that Piet Snyman wanted to know. It was noticeable that Koenrad's condition did not improve very fast.

Nevertheless, his periods of delirium grew fewer, and the number of his visitors dwindled. Towards the end only the ouderling and I were left. And we began discussing, cautiously, the mystery of Frik Engelbrecht's disappearance.

'It's funny about those red flowers on the grass,' the ouderling said in a whisper, when Koenrad was asleep, 'I wonder if he meant that there was blood on the grass?'

We also said that Lettie seemed to be acting strangely, and I said I wondered how she felt about the fact that her lover had not returned.

'Perhaps she has already got her eyes on some other man,' the ouderling said, and he pushed out his chest, and stroked his breast. 'Perhaps what she wants now is an older man, with more understanding. A man who has been married before.'

The ouderling was a widower.

I thought he was talking very foolishly. For it was easy to see – from the look of patient dignity that passed over her face whenever she glanced at me – that Lettie preferred the kind of man that I was.

Then, one day, when Koenrad Wium was well enough to be able to move about the room, two men came for him. One wore a policeman's uniform. The other was in plainclothes, and walked with a brisk step. And Lettie opened the door for them and led them into the bedroom very calmly, as though she had been expecting them.

Bushveld Romance

It's a queer thing – Oom Schalk Lourens observed – how much trouble people will take to hide their weaknesses from the world. Often, of course, they aren't weaknesses at all; only the people who have these peculiarities don't know that. Another thing they don't know is that the world is aware all the time of these things that they imagine they are concealing. I remember a story my grandfather used to tell of something that happened when he was a boy.

Of course, that was a long time ago. It was before the Great Trek. But it seems that even in those days there was trouble between the Boers and English. It had a lot to do with slaves. The English Government wanted to free the slaves, my grandfather said, and one man who was very prominent at the meetings that were held to protest against this was Gert van Tonder.

Now, Gert van Tonder was a very able man and a good speaker; he was at his best, too, when dealing with a subject that he knew nothing at all about. He always spoke very loudly then. You can see that he was a fine leader. So, when the slaves were freed and a manifesto was drawn up to be sent to the King of England, the farmers of Graaff-Reiner took it first to Gert van Tonder for his signature.

You can imagine how surprised everybody was when he refused to sign. They didn't know until long afterwards that it was because he couldn't write. He sat with the manifesto in front of him, and the pen in his hand, and said that he had changed his mind. He said that perhaps they were a bit hasty in writing to the King of England about so trivial a matter.

'Even though the slaves are free, now,' he said, 'it doesn't make any difference. Just let one of my slaves try to act as though he's a free slave, and I'll show him. That's all, just let him try.'

The farmers told Gert van Tonder that he was quite right.

It didn't really make any difference whether the slaves were free or whether they weren't. But they said that they knew that already. There were a lot of other grievances on the manifesto, they explained, and they were sending it to let the King of England know that unless the Boers got their wrongs redressed they would trek out of Cape Colony.

My grandfather used to say that everybody was still more surprised when Gert van Tonder put down the pen, very firmly, and told the farmers that they could trek right to the other end of Africa, for all he cared. He was quite satisfied with the way the King of England did things, Gert said, and there was a lot about English rule for which they had to be thankful. He said that when he was in Cape Town, some months back, at the Castle, he saw an English soldier leave his post to go and kick a coloured man; he said this gave him a respect for the English that he had never had before. He said that, for somebody who couldn't have been in the country very long, that soldier made an extraordinarily good job of assaulting a coloured person.

The upshot of it all was that, when the farmers of the Cape Colony trekked into the North, with their heavily laden wagons and their long spans of oxen and their guns, Gert van Tonder did not go with them. By that time he was saying that another thing they had to be thankful for was the British navy.

My grandfather often spoke about how small a thing it was that kept Gert van Tonder from being remembered in history as one of the leaders of the nation. And it was all just on account of that one weakness of his – of not wanting people to know that he couldn't read or write.

When I talk of people and their peculiarities it always makes me think of Stoffel Lemmer. He had a weakness that was altogether of a different sort. What was peculiar about Stoffel Lemmer was that if a girl or a woman so much as looked at him he was quite certain that she was in love with him. And what made it worse was that he never had the courage to go up and talk to the girl that he thought was making eyes at him.

Another queer thing about Stoffel Lemmer was that he

was just as much in love with the girl as he imagined she was with him. There was that time when that new schoolteacher arrived from somewhere in the Cape. The schoolteacher we had before that had to leave because he was soft in the head. He was always talking about co-operation between parent and teacher, and he used to encourage the parents to call round at the school building just so that everybody could feel friendly.

At first nobody accepted the invitation: the farmers of Drogevlei were diffident about it, and suspicious. But afterwards one or two of them went, and then more of them, until in the end things got very disgraceful. That was when some of the parents, including Piet Terblans, who had never been to school in his life, started fighting in the classroom over what they should tell the teacher he had to do. Piet Terblans said he had his own ideas about how children should be taught, and he couldn't do his work properly if the other parents kept on interrupting him. He used to drive in to school with the children every morning in the donkey wagon and he took his lunch with him.

Then one day shortly after the inspector had called the teacher left. Because when the inspector walked into the classroom he found that the teacher wasn't there at all: he had been pulled out into the passage by several of the rougher parents, who were arguing with him about sums. Instead, when the inspector entered the place, two of the parents were busy drawing on the board with coloured chalks, and Piet Terblans was sitting at the desk, looking very solemn and pretending to write things in the register.

They all said that the teacher was quite well educated and gentlemanly, but soft.

So this time the Education Department sent us a woman schoolteacher. Stoffel Lemmer had been at the Post Office when she arrived. He told me, talking rapidly, that her name was Minnie Bonthuys, and that she had come up from the Cape, and that she had large dark eyes, and that she was in love with him.

'I was standing in the doorway,' Stoffel Lemmer explained, 'and so it wasn't easy for her to get into the voorkamer. As you know, it is only a small door. She stopped and looked at me without speaking. It was almost as though she looked right through me. She looked me up and down, from my head to my feet, I might say. And then she held her chin up very high. And for that reason I knew that she was in love with me. Every girl that's in love with me looks at me like that. Then she went into the voorkamer sideways, because I was standing in the door; and as she passed she drew her skirts close about her. I expect she was afraid that some of the dust that had got on her frock from the motor lorry might shake off on to my khaki trousers. She was very polite. And the first thing she said when she got inside was that she had heard, in Zeerust, that the Groot Marico is a very good district for pigs.'

Stoffel Lemmer went on to say that Piet Terblans, who, out of habit, had again brought his lunch with him, was also there. He said that just before then Piet Terblans had been very busy explaining to the others that he was going to co-operate even more with the new schoolteacher than he had done with the last one.

Nevertheless, when the new schoolteacher walked into the Post Office – Stoffel Lemmer said – Piet Terblans didn't mention anything to her about his ideas on education. Stoffel Lemmer said he didn't know why. It appears that Piet Terblans got as far as clearing his throat several times, as though preparing to introduce himself and his plan to Minnie Bonthuys. But after that he gave it up and ate his lunch instead.

Later on, when I saw the new schoolteacher, I was able to understand quite easily why Stoffel Lemmer had fallen in love with her. I could also understand why Piet Terblans didn't manage to interest her very much in the co-operation scheme that had ended up with the previous teacher having to leave the bushveld. There was no doubt about Minnie Bonthuys being very good-looking, with a lot of black hair that was done up in ringlets. But she had a determined mouth. And in her big dark eyes there was an expression whose meaning was perfectly clear to me. I could see that Minnie Bonthuys knew her own mind and that she was very sure of herself.

As the days passed, Stoffel Lemmer's infatuation for the young schoolteacher increased, and he came and spoke to me about it, as was his custom whenever he fancied himself in love with a girl. So I didn't take much notice of the things he said. I had heard them all so often before.

'I saw her again this morning, Oom Schalk,' he said to me on one occasion. 'I was passing the schoolroom and I was saying her name over to myself, softly. I know I'll never have the courage to go up to her and tell her how I – how I think about her. It's always like that with me, Oom Schalk. I can never bring myself to the point of telling a girl that I love her. Or even saying anything at all to her. I get too frightened somehow. But I saw her this morning Oom Schalk. I went and leant over the barbed wire fence, and I saw her standing in front of the window looking out. I saw her quite a while before she saw me, so that by the time she turned her gaze towards me I was leaning more than half-way over the barbed wire fence.'

Stoffel Lemmer shook his head sadly.

'And I could see by that look in her eyes that she loved me, Oom Schalk,' he went on, 'and by the firm way that her mouth shut when she caught sight of me. In fact, I can hardly even say that she looked at me. It all happened so quickly. She just gave one glance in my direction and then slammed down the window. All girls who are in love with me do just that.'

For some moments Stoffel Lemmer remained silent. He seemed to be thinking.

'I would have gone on standing there, Oom Schalk,' he ended up in a far-away sort of voice. 'Only I couldn't see her any more, because of the way that the sun was shining on the window panes. And I only noticed afterwards how much of the barbed wire had been sticking into me.'

This is just one example of the sort of thing that Stoffel Lemmer would relate to me, sitting on my stoep. Mostly it was in the evening. And he would look out into the dusk and say that the shadows that lay on the thorn trees were in his heart also. As I have told you, I had so frequently heard him say exactly the same thing. About other girls.

And always he would end up in the same way – saying what a sorrowful thing it was that he would never be able to tell her how much he loved her. He also said how grateful he was to have somebody who could listen to his sad story with understanding. That one, too, I had heard before. Often.

What's that? Did he ever tell her? Well, I don't know. The last time I saw Stoffel Lemmer was in Zeerust. It was in front of the church, after the ceremony. And by the determined expression that Minnie still had on her face when the wedding guests threw rice and confetti over Stoffel and herself – no, I don't think he ever got up the courage to tell her.

Concertinas and Confetti

Hendrik Uys and I were boys together (Oom Schalk Lourens said). At school we were also class-mates. That is, if you can call it being class-mates, seeing that our relationship was that we sat together at the same desk, and that Hendrik Uys, who was three years older than I, used to sit almost on top of me so as to make it easier for him to copy off me. And whenever I got an answer wrong Hendrik Uys used to get very annoyed, because it meant that he also got caned for doing bad work, and after we got caned he always used to kick me after we got outside the school.

'This will teach you to pay attention to the teacher when he is talking,' Hendrik Uys used to say to me when we were on our way home. 'You ought to be ashamed of yourself, when your father is making all these sacrifices to keep you at school. You got two sums wrong and you made three mistakes in spelling today.' And after that he would start kicking me.

And the strange thing is that what he said really made me feel sad, and I felt that in making mistakes in spelling and sums I was throwing away my opportunities, and when he spoke about my father's sacrifices to give me an education I felt that Hendrik Uys was a good son who had fine feelings towards his parents, and it never occurred to me at the time that in not doing any work of his own but just copying down everything I wrote – that in that respect Hendrik Uys was a lot more ungrateful than I was. In fact, it was only years later that it struck me that in carrying on in the way he was Hendrik Uys was displaying a most unpraiseworthy kind of contempt for his own parents' sacrifices.

And because he spoke so touchingly about my father I had a deep respect for Hendrik Uys. There were no limits to my admiration for him.

Yet afterwards, when I grew up, I found that real life amongst grown-up people was not so very different from what went on in that little schoolroom with the white-washed walls, and the wooden step that had been worn hollow by the passage of hundreds of little feet including the somewhat larger veldskoened feet of Hendrik Uys. And the delicate green of the rosyntjie-bush that grew just to the side of the school-building within convenient reach of the penknife of the Hollander schoolmaster, who went out and cut a number of thick but supple canes every morning just after the Bible lesson, before the more strenuous work of the day started.

And I remember how always, after we had been caned for getting wrong answers, Hendrik Uys would walk down the road with me, rubbing the places where the rosyntjie-bush cane had fallen, and calling the schoolmaster a useless, fat-faced, squint-eyed Hollander. But shortly afterwards he would turn on me and upbraid me, and he would say he could not understand how I could have the heart, through my slothfulness, to bring such sorrow to the grey hairs of a poor schoolmaster who already had one foot in the grave.

And as if to emphasise this last statement about its being the schoolmaster's foot that was in the grave, Hendrik Uys would proceed, with each foot alternately, to kick me.

Yes, I suppose you could say that Hendrik was a school-friend of mine.

And once when my father asked him how we got on in school, Hendrik said that it was all right. Only there was rather a lot of copying going on. And he looked meaningly in my direction. Hendrik Uys was so convincing that it was impossible for me to try and tell my father the truth. Instead, I just kept silent and felt very much ashamed of myself. I suppose it is because of what the term 'school-friend' implies that I am glad that our schooling did not last very long in those days.

If he had continued in that way after he had grown up, and had applied to practical life the knowledge of the world which he had acquired in the classroom there is no doubt that Hendrik Uys would have gone far. I feel sure that he would at least have got elected to the Volksraad.

But when he was a young man something happened to Hendrik Uys that changed him completely. He fell in love with Marie Snyman, and his whole life became different.

I don't think I have ever witnessed so amazing a change in any person as what came over Hendrik Uys in his late twenties when he first discovered that he was in love with Marie Snyman, a dark-haired girl with a low, soft voice and quiet eyes that never seemed to look at you, but that appeared to gaze inwards, always, as though she was looking at frail things. There was a disturbing sort of wisdom in her eyes, shadowy, something like the knowledge that the past has of a future that is made of dust.

'I can't understand how I could have been such a fool,' Hendrik Uys said to us one day while we were drinking coffee in the dining room of the new post office. 'To think that Marie Snyman was at school with me, and that I never saw her, even, if you know what I mean. She seemed just an ordinary girl to me, with thin legs and her hair in plaits. And she has been living here, in these parts, all these years, and it is only now that I have found her. I wasted all these years when the one woman in my life has been living here, right amonst us, all the time. It seems so foolish, I feel like kicking myself.'

When Hendrik Uys spoke those last words about kicking, I moved uneasily on my chair for a moment. Although my school-days were far in the past, there were still certain painful memories that lingered.

'But I must have been in love with her even then, without knowing it,' Hendrik Uys went on, 'otherwise I wouldn't have remembered her plaits. Ordinary-looking plaits they seemed, too. Stringy.'

'The postcart with the letters is late,' Theunis Bekker said, yawning.

'And her thin legs,' Hendrik Uys continued.

'Perhaps the postcart had trouble getting through the Groen River,' Adrian Schoeman said, 'I hear it has been raining in Zeerust.'

'Maybe love is like that,' Hendrik Uys went on 'it's there a long time, but you don't always know it.'

'The postcart may be stuck in the mud,' Theunis Bekker said, yawning again, 'the turf beyond Sephton's Nek is all thick, slimy mud when it rains.'

'But her eyes weren't like that then, when she was at school,' Hendrik Uys finished up lamely. 'You know what her eyes are like – quiet, sort of.'

His voice trailed off into silence.

And if a great change had come over Hendrik Uys when he fell in love with Marie Snyman, it was nothing compared with the way in which he changed after they were married. For up to that time Hendrik Uys had abundantly fulfilled the promise of his school-days. He had been appointed a diaken of the Dutch Reformed Church and he was a prominent committee member of the Farmers' Association and the part he was playing in politics was already of such a character as to make more than one person regard him as a prospective candidate for the Volksraad in a few years' time.

And then, I suppose, like every other Volksraad member, he would pay a visit to his old school some day, and he would talk to the teacher and the children and he would tell them that in that same classroom, where the teacher had been a kindly old Hollander, long since dead, the foundation of his public career had been laid. And that he had got into the Volksraad simply through having applied the sound knowledge which he had acquired in the school.

Which would no doubt have been true enough.

But after he had fallen in love with Marie Snyman, Hendrik Uys changed altogether. For one thing, he resigned his position as diaken of the Dutch Reformed Church. This was a shock to everybody, because it was a very honoured position, and many envied him for having received the appointment at so early an age. Then, when he explained the reason for his resignation, the farmers in the neighbourhood were still more shocked.

What Hendrik Uys said was that since he had found Marie Snyman he had been so altered by the purity of her love for him that from now on he wanted to do only honest things. He wanted to be worthy of her love, he said.

'And I used unfair means to get the appointment as diaken,' Hendrik Uys explained. 'I got it through having induced the predikant to use his influence on my behalf. I had made the predikant a present of two trek-oxen just at that time, when it was uncertain whether the appointment would go to me or to Hans van Tonder.'

They were married in the church in Zeerust. Hendrik Uys and Marie Snyman, and that part of the wedding made us feel very uncomfortable, for it was obvious by the sneer that the predikant wore on his face throughout the religious ceremony that he had certain secret reservations about how he thought the marriage was going to turn out. It was obvious that the predikant had been told the reason for Hendrik's resignation as diaken.

But the reception afterwards made up for a lot of the unhappier features of the church ceremony. The guests were seated at long tables in the grounds of the hotel, and when one of the waiters shouted 'Aan die brand!' as a signal to the band-leader, and the strains of the concertina and the guitars swept across our hearts, thrillingly, like a sudden wind through the grass, and the bride and bridegroom entered, the bride wearing a white satin dress with a long train, and there was confetti in Marie's hair and on Hendrik's shoulders – oh, well it was all so very beautiful. And it seemed sad that life could not always be like that. It seemed a pity that life was not satisfied to let us always bear on our shoulders things only as light as confetti.

And as a kind of gesture to Hendrik, to let him sort of see that I was prepared to let schooldays be bygones, when the bride and bridegroom drove off on their honeymoon I was the one that flung the old veldskoen after them.

Afterwards, when I was inspanning to go back to the bushveld, I saw the predikant. I was still thinking about life. By that time I was wondering why it was that we always had to carry in our hearts things that were so much heavier than concertina music borne on the wind. The predikant was talking to a number of Marico farmers grouped around him. And because that sneer was still on his face I could see that the predikant was talking about Hendrik Uys. So I walked nearer.

'He resigned as diaken because he said he bribed me with a couple of trek-oxen,' I heard the predikant say. 'I wonder what does he take me for? Does he think I am an Evangelist or an Apostolic pastor that I can be bribed with a couple of trek-oxen? And those beasts were as thin as cows. Man, they went for next to nothing on the Johannesburg market.'

The men listening to the predikant nodded gravely.

This was the beginning of Hendrik Uys's unpopularity in the Marico bushveld. It wasn't that Hendrik and Marie were avoided by people, or anything like that; it was just that it came to be recognised that the two of them seemed to prefer to live alone as much as possible. And, of course, there was nothing unfriendly about it all. Only, it seemed strange to me that as long as Hendrik Uys had been cunning and active in pushing his own interests, without being much concerned as to whether the means he employed were right or wrong, he appeared to be generally liked. But when he started becoming honest and overscrupulous in his dealings with others, then it seemed that people did not have the same kind of affection for him.

I saw less and less of Hendrik and Marie as the years went by. They had a daughter whom they christened Annette. And after that they had no more children. Hendrik made one or two further attempts to get reappointed as a diaken. He also spoke vaguely of having political ambitions. But it was clear that his heart was no longer in public or social activities. And on those occasions on which I saw him he spoke mostly of his love for his wife, Marie. And he spoke much of how the years had not changed their love. And he said that his greatest desire in life was that his daughter, Annette, should grow up like her mother and make a loyal and gentle and loving wife to a man who would be worthy of her love.

I remembered how Hendrik had spoken about Marie, years before in the post office, when they were first thinking of getting married. And I remembered how he spoke of that stillness that seemed to be so deep a part of her nature. And Hendrik's wife did not seem to change with the passage of the years. She always moved about the house very quietly, and when she spoke it was usually with downcast eyes, and whether she was working or sitting at rest on the riempies bench, what seemed to come all the time out of her whole personality was a strange and very deep kind of stillness. And the quiet that flowed out of her body did not appear to be like that calmness that comes to one after grief, that tranquility of the spirit that follows on weeping, but it had in it more of the quality of that other stillness, like when at high noon the veld is still.

I knew that it was this quiet that Hendrik loved above all in his wife Marie, and when he spoke of his daughter Annette – and he spoke of her in such a way that it was clear that he was devoting his whole life to the vision of his daughter growing up to be exactly like her mother – I always knew what that quality was that he looked to find in his daughter, Annette. Even when he never mentioned it in actual words.

Annette grew up to be a very pretty girl, a lot like her mother in looks, and when it came to her turn to be married, it was to Koos de Bruyn, a wealthy farmer from Rustenburg. For her wedding in the church in Zeerust, Annette wore the same wedding dress of white satin that her mother had worn twenty years before, and I was surprised to see how little the material had yellowed. It was pleasing to think that there were things that throughout those many years remained unchanged.

And when Annette came out of the church after the ceremony, leaning on her husband's arm, and there was confetti in her hair and on his shoulder I knew then that it was not only in respect of the white satin dress that there was a similarity between the marriage of Annette and that of her mother twenty years before. And I knew that that depth of stillness that Hendrik had loved in his wife would form a part of his daughter's nature, also. And the spirit to Annette for the rest of her married life. And in that way I guessed what had caused it as well in the case of her mother, Marie, the wife of Hendrik. And I wondered whether Annette's husband would love that quality in her, also.

It was a very slight thing. And it was so very quick that one would hardly have noticed it, even. It was just that something that came into her eyes – so apparently insignificant that it might have been no more than the trembling of an eyelash, almost – when Annette tripped out of the church, leaning on her husband's arm, and she glanced swiftly at a young man with broad shoulders whose very white face was half turned away.

The Story of Hester van Wyk

When I think of the story of Hester van Wyk I often wonder what is it about some stories that I have wanted to tell (Oom Schalk Lourens said). About things that have happened and about people that I have known – and that I still know, some of them: if you can call it knowing a person when your mule-carts pass each other on the Government road, and you wave your hat cheerfully and call out that it will be a good season for the crops, if only the stalk-borers and other pests keep away, and the other person just nods at you, with a distant sort of look in his eyes, and says, yes, the Marico Bushveld has unfortunately got more than one kind of pest.

That was what Gawie Steyn said to me one afternoon on the Government road, when I was on my way to the Drogedal post office for letters and he was on his way home. And it was because of the sorrowful sort of way in which he uttered the word 'unfortunately' that I knew that Gawie Steyn had heard what I said about him to Frik Prinsloo three weeks before, after the meeting of the Dwarsberg debating society in the schoolroom next to the poort.

In any case, I never finished that story that I told Frik Prinsloo about Gawie Steyn, although I began telling it colourfully enough that night after the meeting of the debating society was over and the farmers and their wives and children had all gone home, and Frik Prinsloo and I were sitting alone on two desks in the middle of the schoolroom, with our feet up, and our pipes pleasantly filled with strong plug-cut tobacco whose thick blue fumes made the school-teacher cough violently at intervals.

The schoolmaster was seated at his table, with his head in his hands, and his face looking very pale in the light of the one paraffin lamp. And he was waiting for us to leave so that he could blow out his lamp and lock up the schoolroom and go home.

The schoolmaster did not interrupt us only with his coughing but also in other ways. For instance, he told us on several occasions that he had a weak chest, and if we had made up our minds to stay on like this in the classroom, talking, after the meeting was over, would we mind very much, he asked, if he opened one of the windows to let out some of the blue clouds of tobacco smoke.

But Frik Prinsloo said that we would mind very much. Not for our sakes, Frik said, but for the schoolmaster's sake. There was nothing worse, Frik explained, than for a man with a weak chest to sit in a room with a window open.

'It is nothing for us,' Frik Prinsloo said, 'for Schalk Lourens and myself to sit in a room with an open window. We are two bushveld farmers with sturdy physiques who have been through the Boer War and through the anthrax pestilence. We have survived not only human hardships, but also cattle and sheep and pig diseases. At Magersfontein I even slept in an aardvark hole that was half-full of water with a piece of newspaper tied around my left ankle for the rheumatism. And even so neither Schalk Lourens nor I will be so foolish as to be in a room that has got a window open.'

'No,' I agreed. 'Never.'

'And you have to take greater care of your health than any of us,' Frik Prinsloo said to the schoolteacher. 'With your weak chest it would be dangerous for you to have a window open in here. Why, you can't even stand our tobacco smoke. Look at the way you are coughing right now.'

After he had knocked the ash out of his pipe into an inkwell that was let into a little round hole in one of the desks, an action which he had performed just in order to show how familiar, for an uneducated man, he was with the ways of a schoolroom, Frik started telling the schoolteacher about other places he had slept in, both during the Boer War and at another time when he was doing transportriding.

Frik Prinsloo embarked on a description of the hardships of a transportrider's life in the old days. It was a story that seemed longer than the most ambitious journey ever undertaken by ox-wagon, and much heavier, and more roundabout. And there was one place where Frik Prinsloo's story got stuck much more hopelessly than any of his ox-wagons had ever got stuck in a drift.

Then the schoolmaster said, please, gentlemen, he could not stand it any more. His health was bad, and while he could perhaps arrange to let us have the use of the schoolroom on some other night, so that I could finish the story that I appeared to be telling to Mr. Prinsloo, and he would even provide the paraffin for the lamp himself, he really had to go home and get some sleep.

But Frik Prinsloo said the schoolmaster did not need to worry about the paraffin. We would sit just as comfortably in the dark and talk, he said. For that matter, the schoolmaster could go to sleep in the classroom, if he liked. Just like that, sitting at the table.

'You already look half asleep,' Frik told him, winking at me, 'and sleeping in a schoolroom is a lot better than what happened to me during the English advance on Bloemfontein, when I slept in a donga with a lot of slime and mud and slippery tadpoles at the bottom.'

'In a donga half-full of water with a piece of mealie-sacking fastened around your stomach because of the colic,' the schoolteacher said, speaking with his head still between his hands. 'And for heaven's sake, if you have got to sleep out on the veld, why don't you sleep on top of it? Why must you go and lie inside a hole full of water or inside a slimy donga? If you farmers have had hard lives, it seems to me that you yourselves did quite a lot to make them like that.'

We ignored this remark of the schoolmaster's which we both realised was based on his lack of worldly experience, and I went on to relate to Frik Prinsloo those incidents from the life of Gawie Steyn that were responsible for Gawie's talking about Marico pests, some weeks later, in gloomy tones, on the road winding between the thorn trees to the post office.

And this was one of those stories that I never finished. Because the schoolmaster fell asleep at his table, with the result that he didn't cough any more, and I could see that because of this Frik Prinsloo could not derive the same amount of amusement from my story. And what is even more strange is that I also found that the funny parts in the story did not sound so funny any more, now that the schoolmaster was no longer in discomfort. The story seemed to have had much more life in it, somehow, in the earlier stages, when the schoolmaster was anxiously waiting for us to go home, and coughing at intervals through the blue haze of our tobacco smoke.

'And so that man came round again the next night and sang more songs to Gawie Steyn's wife,' I said, 'and they were old songs that he sang.'

'It sounds to me as though he is even snoring,' Frik Prinsloo said. 'Imagine that for ill-bred. Here are you telling a story that teaches one all about the true and deep things of life and the schoolmaster is lying with his head on the table, snoring.'

'And when Gawie Steyn started objecting after a while,' I continued, with a certain amount of difficulty, 'the man said the excuse he had to offer was that they were all old songs, anyway, and they didn't mean very much. Old songs had no meaning. They were only dead things from the past. They were yellowed and dust-laden, the man said.'

'I've got a good mind to wake him,' Frik Prinsloo went on. 'First he disturbs us with his coughing and now I can't hear what you're saying because of his snoring. It will be a good thing if we just go home and leave him. He seems so attached to his schoolroom. Even staying behind at night to sleep in it. What would people say if I liked ploughing so much that I didn't go home at night, but just lay down and slept on a strip of grass next to a furrow?'

'Then Gawie Steyn said to this man,' I continued, with greater difficulty than ever before, 'he said that it wasn't so much the old songs he objected to. The old songs might be well enough. But the way his wife listened to the songs, he said, seemed to him to be not so much like an old song as like an old story.'

'Not that I don't sleep out on the lands sometimes,' Frik Prinsloo explained, 'and even in the ploughing season. But then it is in the early afternoon of a hot day. And the kafirs go on with the ploughing all the same. And it is very refreshing then, to sleep under a withaak tree knowing that the kafirs are at work in the sun. Sleeping on a strip of green grass next to a furrow . . .'

'Or inside the furrow,' the schoolmaster said, and we only noticed then that he was no longer snoring. 'Inside a furrow half-filled with wet fertilizer and with a turnip fastened on your head because of the blue tongue.'

As I have said, this story about Gawie Steyn and his wife is one of those stories that I never finished telling. And I would never have known, either, that Frik Prinsloo had listened to as much of it as I had told him, if it wasn't for Gawie Steyn's manner of greeting me on the Government road, three weeks later, with sorrowful politeness, like an Englishman.

There is always something unusual about a story that does not come to an end on its own. It is as though that story keeps going on, getting told in a different way each time, as though the story itself is trying to find out what happened next.

It was like the way life came to Hester van Wyk.

Hester was a very pretty girl, with black hair and a way of smiling that seemed very childlike, until you were close enough to her to see what was in her eyes, and then you realised, in that same moment, that no child had ever smiled like that. And whether it was for her black hair or whether it was because of her smile, it so happened that Hester van Wyk was hardly ever without a lover. They came to her, the young men from the neighbourhood. But they also went away again. They tarried for a while, like birds in their passage, and they paid court to her, and sometimes the period in which they wooed her was quite long, and at other times again she would have a lover whose ardour seemed to last for no longer than a few brief weeks before he also went his way.

And it seemed that the story of Hester van Wyk and her lovers was also one of those stories that I have mentioned to you, whose end never gets told.

And Gert van Wyk, Hester's father, would talk to me about these young men that came into his daughter's life. He talked to me both as a neighbour and as a relative on his wife's side, and while what he said to me about Hester and her lovers were mostly words spoken lightly, in the way that you flick a pebble into a dam, and watch the yellow ripples widening, there were also times when he spoke differently. And then what he said was like the way a footsore wanderer flings his pack on to the ground

'She's a pretty girl,' Gert said to me. 'Yes, she is pretty enough. But her trouble is that she is too soft-hearted. These young men come to her, and they tell her stories. Sad stories about their lives. And she listens to their stories. And she feels sorry for them. And she says that they must be very nice young men for life to have treated them so badly. She even tries to tell me some of these stories, so that I should also feel sorry for them. But, of course, I have got too much sense to listen. I simply tell her –'

'Yes,' I answered, nodding. 'you tell her that what the young man says is a lot of lies. And by the time you have convinced her about one lover's lies you find that he has already departed, and that some other young man has got into the habit of coming to your house three times a week, and that he is busy telling her a totally new and different story.'

'That's what he imagines,' Gert van Wyk replies, 'that it's new. But it's always the same old story. Only, instead of telling of his unhappy childhood the new young man will talk about his aged mother, or about how life has been cruel to him, so that he has got to help on the farm, for which he isn't suited at all, because it makes him dizzy to have to pump water out of the borehole for the cattle – up and down, up and down, like that, with the pump-handle – when all the time his real ambition is to have the job of wearing a blue and gold uniform outside of a bioscope in Johannesburg. And my daughter Hester is so soft-hearted that she goes on listening to these same stupid stories day after day, year in and year out.'

'Yes,' I said, 'they are the same old stories.'

And I thought of what Gawie Steyn said about the man who sang old songs to his wife. And it seemed that Hester van Wyk's was also an old story, and that for that reason it would never end.

'Did she also have a young man who said that he was not

worthy of her because he was not educated?' I asked Gert. 'And did she take pity on him because he said people looked down on him because of his table manners?'

'Yes,' Gert answered with alacrity, 'he said he was badly brought up and always forgot to take the teaspoon out of the cup before drinking his coffee.'

'Did she also have a young man who got her sympathy by telling her that he had fallen in love years ago, and that he had lost that girl, because her parents had objected to him, and that he could never fall in love again?'

'Quite right,' Gert said, 'this young man said that his first girl's parents refused to let her marry him because his forehead was too low. Even though he tried to make it look higher by training his eyebrows down and shaving the hair off most of the top of his head. But how do you know all these things?'

'There are only a few stories that young men tell girls in order to get their sympathy,' I said to Gert. 'There are only a handful of stories like that. But it seems to me that your daughter Hester has been told them all. And more than once, too, sometimes, by the look of it.'

'And you can imagine how awful that young man with the low forehead looked,' Gert continued. 'He must have been unattractive enough before. But with his eyebrows trained down and the top of his head shaved clean off, he looked more like a –'

'And for that very reason, of course,' I explained, 'your daughter Hester fell in love with him. After she had heard his story.'

And it seemed to me that the oldest story of all must be the story of a woman's heart.

It was some years after this, when Gert van Wyk and his family had moved out of the Marico into the Waterberg, that I heard that Hester van Wyk had married. And I knew then what had happened, of course. And I knew it even without Gert having had to tell me.

I knew then that some young man must have come to Hester van Wyk from out of some far-lying part of the Waterberg. He came to her and found her. And in finding her he had no story to tell.

But what I have no means of telling, now that I have related to you all that I know, is whether this is the end of the story about Hester van Wyk.

Campfires at Nagmaal

Of course, the old days, were best (Oom Schalk Lourens said), I mean the really old days. Those times when we still used to pray, 'Lord give us food and clothes. The veldskoens we make ourselves.'

There was faith in the land in those days. And when things went wrong we used to rely on our own hands and wills, and when we asked for the help of the Lord we also knew the strength of our trek-chains. It was quite a few years before the Boer War that what I can call the old days came to an end. That was when the Boers in these parts stopped making the soles of their veldskoens out of strips of raw leather that they cut from quagga skins. Instead, they started using the new kind of blue sole that came up from the Cape in big square pieces, and that they bought at the Indian store.

I remember the first time I made myself a pair of veldskoens out of that blue sole. The stuff was easy to work with, and smooth. And all the time I was making the veldskoens I knew it was very wrong. And I was still more disappointed when I found that the blue sole wore well. If anything, it was even better than raw quagga hide. This circumstance was very regrettable to me. And there remained something foreign to me about those veldskoens, even after they had served me through two kafir wars.

It was in the early days, also, that a strange set of circumstances unfolded, in which the lives of three people. Maans Prinsloo and Stoffelina Lemmer and Petrus Steyn, became intertwined like the strands of the grass covers that native women weave for their beer-pots: in some places your eye can separate the various strands of plaited grass, the one from the other; in other places the weaving is all of one piece.

And the story of the lives of these three people, two men and a girl, is something that could only have happened long ago, when there was still faith in the Transvaal, and the stars in the sky were constant, and only the wind changed.

Maans Prinsloo and I were young men together, and I knew Stoffelina Lemmer well, also. But because Petrus Steyn, who was a few years older than we were, lived some distance away, to the north, on the borders of the Bechuanaland Protectorate, I did not see him very often. We met mostly at Nagmaals, and then Petrus Steyn would recount to us, at great length, the things he had seen and the events that had befallen him on his periodical treks into the further parts of the Kalahari desert.

You can imagine that these stories of Petrus Steyn's were very tedious to listen to. They were empty as the desert is, and as unending. And as flat.

After all, it is easy to understand that Petrus Steyn's visits to the Kalahari desert would not give him very much to talk about that would be of interest to the listener – no matter how far he trekked. Simply because a desert is a desert. One part of it is exactly like another part. Thousands of square miles of sand dotted with occasional thorn-trees. And a stray buck or two. And, now and again, a few Bushmen who have also strayed – but who don't know it, of course.

I have noticed that Bushmen are always in a hurry. But they have nowhere to go to. Where they are running to is all just desert, like where they came from. So they never know where they are, either. But because they don't care where they are it doesn't matter to them that they are lost. They just don't know any better. All they are concerned about is to keep on hurrying.

Consequently, the stories that Petrus Steyn had to tell of his experiences in the Kalahari desert were as fatiguing to listen to as if you were actually trekking along with him. And the further he trekked into the desert the more wearisome his narrative became, on account of the interludes getting fewer, there being less buck and less Bushmen the deeper he got into the interior. Even so, we felt that he was keeping on using the same Bushmen over and over again. There was also a small herd of springbok that we were suspicious about in the same way.

You can picture to yourself the scene around one of the fires on the church square in Zeerust. It happened at many Nagmaals. A number of young men and women seated around the fire, and Petrus Steyn, a few years older than the members of his audience, would be talking. And when you saw people's mouths going open, it wasn't in astonishment. They were just yawning.

But there was one reason why the young men and women came to Petrus Steyn, and this reason had nothing to do with his Kalahari stories. But it is one of the things I was thinking about when I spoke about the old days and about the faith that was in the land then. For Petrus Steyn was regarded as a prophet. Sometimes people believed in his prognostications, and sometimes they didn't. But, of course, this made no difference to Petrus Steyn. He didn't care whether or not his prophecies came out. He believed in them just the same. More, even. You would understand whan I mean by this if you knew Petrus Steyn.

And Petrus Steyn said that why he went into the Kalahari periodically was in order to get fresh inspiration and guidance in regard to the future. He also said it was written in the Bible that a prophet had to go into the desert.

'I wonder what the Bushmen thought of Zephaniah, when he was in the desert,' Maans Prinsloo asked, 'I suppose they painted portraits of him, on rocks.'

Maans Prinsloo knew the Zephaniah was Petrus Steyn's favourite prophet.

'I don't know whether Ekron was rooted up, like Zephaniah said would happen,' Petrus Steyn replied, 'I read the Bible right through to Revelations, once, to find out. But I couldn't be sure if Zephaniah was right or not. That's where my prophecies are different. When I see a thing in the Kalahari desert, that thing comes out, no matter who gets struck down by it' – and Petrus Steyn looked sternly at Maans Prinsloo – 'and no matter how long it takes.'

That was how Petrus Steyn always talked about his prophecies. And maybe that was the reason why they believed in him, even when they should not have done so.

Anyway, I can still recall, very clearly, that particular Nagmaal at Zeerust when I first understood in which way Stoffelina Lemmer came into the story. And I also knew why Maans Prinsloo and Petrus Steyn were on unfriendly terms. Stoffelina Lemmer had dark hair, and eyes that had a far-off light in them when she smiled, and that were strangely shadowed when she looked at you without smiling. And she had red lips.

Stoffelina Lemmer was much in Maans Prinsloo's company at this Nagmaal. But she was also a great deal with Petrus Steyn. She was nearly always one of the little group that listened to Petrus Steyn's Kalahari stories, and even if Maans Prinsloo was with her, holding her hand, even, it still seemed that she listened to Petrus Steyn's talk. That is, she appeared, unlike anybody else, actually to listen, and with an interest that was not simulated.

Once or twice, also, after the rest of Petrus Steyn's audience had departed, it was observed that Stoffelina Lemmer remained behind, talking to the prophet. And to judge by the animation of Stoffelina Lemmer's lips and eyes, if they were talking about the future it was not in terms of Petrus Steyn's desert prophecies. Beside the burnt-out campfire they lingered thus, once or twice; Stoffelina and Petrus, with the dull glow of the dying embers on their faces.

It was only reasonable, therefore, that Maans Prinsloo should want to know where he stood with Stoffelina Lemmer. That he was in love with her, everybody knew by this time. It was also known, shortly afterwards, that Maans had asked Stoffelina to marry him. And from the way that Maans Prinsloo walked about, looking disconsolate and making remarks of a slighting nature about the whole of the Kalahari, and not just the parts that Petrus Steyn went into, it was clear to us that Stoffelina Lemmer had not accepted Maans Prinsloo just out of hand.

Then, when it was becoming very tense, this situation that involved two men and a girl, Stoffelina Lemmer found a way out.

'Let Petrus Steyn go out into the desert again, after this Nagmaal,' Stoffelina said. 'And let him then come back and tell us what he has seen. He will learn in the Kalahari what is to happen. When he comes back he will tell us.'

Although he believed in Petrus Steyn's prophecies, in spite of his pretence to the contrary, Maans Prinsloo nevertheless seemed doubtful.

'But, look,' he began, 'Petrus Steyn is sure to go in just a little distance. And then he will come out and say that Stoffelina Lemmer is going to marry Petrus Steyn, and that . . .'

Petrus Steyn silenced Maans Prinsloo with a look.

'I shall trek into the Kalahari desert,' he said. 'It will be the longest journey I have ever made into the desert. And whatever I see will be prophecy. And just as I see it I shall come back and announce it. Zephaniah may prophesy wrongly, dishonestly, even . . . Petrus Steyn, never! I am still not satisfied about what Zephaniah spoke against Ekron.'

Maans Prinsloo was convinced. And so the matter was decided. We inspanned on the Nagmaal plein at Zeerust and journeyed back to our farms by oxwagon, and shortly afterwards we heard that Petrus Steyn had set out on a long trek into the Kalahari desert.

Nothing remained to be told after that Nagmaal at which it was decided that Petrus Steyn should trek into the Kalahari once more. The story ended when the last red ember turned to ashes in that camp-fire on the Nagmaal plein.

Maans Prinsloo remained nervous for a very considerable period.

Because this time Petrus Steyn went on a trip that was longer than anything he had ever undertaken before. In fact, he trekked right across the Kalahari, right through to the other side, and far into Portuguese Angola. Indeed, it was more than fifteen years before we again heard of him, and then it was indirectly, through some Boers who had trekked into Portuguese territory in order to get away from British rule.

I often wondered if those Boers had ever asked Petrus Steyn what it was that he had trekked away from.

But before that time there were many Nagmaals, one succeeding the other, when Stoffelina Lemmer and Maans Prinsloo sat near each other, in front of the same camp-fire, each one waiting, and each one's heart crowded with different emotions,

for the return of Petrus Steyn from the desert.
No, Stoffelina Lemmer never married Maans Prinsloo.

Treasure Trove

It is queer, (Oom Schalk Lourens said), about treasure-hunting. You can actually find the treasure, and through ignorance, or through forgetting to look, at the moment when you have got it, you can let it slip through your fingers like sand. Take Namaqualand, for instance. That part where all those diamonds are lying around, waiting to be picked up. Now they have got it all fenced in, and there are hundreds of police patrolling what we thought, in those days, was just a piece of desert. I remember the last time I trekked through that part of the country, which I took to be an ungodly stretch of sandy waste. But if I had known that I was travelling through thousands of miles of diamond mine, I don't think I would have hurried so much. And that area wouldn't have seemed so very ungodly either.

I made the last part of the journey on foot. And you know how it is when you are walking through the sand; how you have to stop ever so often to sit down and shake out your boots. I get quite a sick feeling, even now, when I think that I never once looked to see what I was shaking out. You hear of a person allowing a fortune to slip through his fingers. But it is much sadder if he lets it trickle away through between the leather of his veldskoens.

Anyway, when the talk comes round to fortunes, and so on, I always call to mind the somewhat singular search that went on, for the better part of a bushveld summer, on Jan Slabbert's farm. We all said, afterwards, that Jan Slabbert should have known better, at his age and experience, than to have allowed a stranger like that callow young Hendrik Buys, on the strength of a few lines drawn on a piece of wrapping paper, to come along and start up so much foolishness.

Jan Slabbert was very mysterious about the whole thing, at first. He introduced Hendrik Buys to us as 'a young man from the Cape who is having a look over my farm.' These words of Jan Slabbert's did not, however, reveal to us much that we did not already know. Indeed, I had on more than one occasion come across Hendrik Buys, unexpectedly and from behind, when he was quite clearly engaged in looking over Jan Slabbert's farm. He had even got down on his hands and knees to look it over better.

But in the end, after several neighbours had unexpectedly come across Jan Slabbert in the same way, he admitted that they were conducting a search for hidden treasure.

'I suppose, because it's hidden treasure, Jan Slabbert thinks that it has got to be kept hidden from us, also,' Jurie Bekker said one day when several of us were sitting in his post office.

'It's a treasure consisting of gold coins and jewels that were buried on Jan Slabbert's farm many years ago,' Neels Erasmus, who was a church elder, explained. 'I called on Jan Slabbert – not because I was inquisitive about the treasure, of course – but in connection with something of a theological character that happened at the last Nagmaal, and Jan Slabbert and Hendrik Buys were both out. They were on the veld.'

'On their hands and knees,' Jurie Bekker said.

The ouderling went on to tell us that Jan Slabbert's daughter, Susannah, had said that a piece of the map which that young fellow, Buys, had brought with him from the Cape, was missing, with the result that they were having difficulty in locating the spot marked with a cross.

'It's always like that with a map of a place where there is buried treasure,' Jurie Bekker said. 'You can follow a lot of directions, until you come to an old tree or an old grave or an old forked road with cobwebs on it, and then you have to take a hundred paces to the west, and then there's something missing –'

'Neels Erasmus, the ouderling, was talking to Susannah,' he said, and his voice sounded kind of rasping. He always liked to be the first with the news. But Jurie Bekker was able to assure us that he had just guessed those details. Every treasure-hunt map was like that, he repeated.

'Well, you got it pretty right,' Neels Erasmus said. 'There is an old tree in it, and an old forked road and an old grave, I think, and also a pair of men's underpants – the long kind. The underpants seem to have been the oldest clue of the whole lot. And it was the underpants that convinced Jan Slabbert that the map was genuine. He was doubtful about it, until then.'

The ouderling went on to say that where this map also differed from the usual run of treasure-trove maps was that you didn't have to pace off one hundred yards to the west in the last stage of trying to locate the spot.

'Instead,' he explained, 'you've got to crawl on your hands and knees for I don't know how far. You see, the treasure was buried at night. And the men that buried it crawled through the bush on hands and knees for the last part of the way.'

We said that from the positions in which we had often seen Jan Slabbert and Hendrik Buys of late, it was clear that they were also on the last part of their search.

Andries Prinsloo, a young man who had all this while been sitting in a corner on a low riempies-stoel, and had until then taken no part in the conversation, suddenly remarked to Neels Erasmus, (and he cleared his throat nervously as he spoke), that it seemed to him as though the ouderling 'and – and Susannah – er – had quite a lot to say to each other.' Perhaps it was because he was respectful of our company that Andries Prinsloo's remark started us off saying all kinds of things of an improving nature.

'Yes,' I said to Neels Erasmus, 'I wonder what your wife would have to say if she knew that you went to call at Jan Slabbert's house when only his daughter, Susannah, was at home.'

'You went in the morning, because you knew that Jan Slabbert and Hendrik Buys would be outside, then, creeping through the wag-'n-bietjie thorns,' Jurie Bekker said. 'The afternoons, of course, they keep free for creeping through the haak-doring thorns.'

'And what will your wife say if she knew of the subjects you discussed with Susannah?' I asked.

'Yes, all those intimate things,' Jurie Bekker continued. 'Like about that pair of old underpants. How could you talk to a young, innocent girl like Susannah about those awful old underp—'

Jurie Bekker spluttered so much that he couldn't get the word out. Then we both broke into loud guffaws. And in the midst of all this laughter, Andries Prinsloo went out very quietly, almost as though he didn't want to disturb us. It seemed that that young fellow had so much respect for our company that he did not wish to take part in anything that might resemble unseemly mirth. And we did not feel like laughing any more, either, somehow, after he had left.

When we again discussed Jan Slabbert's affairs in the post office, the treasure-hunt had reached the stage where a gang of kafirs, under the supervision of the two white men, went from place to place on the farm, digging holes. In some places they even dug tunnels. They found nothing. We said that it would only be somebody like Jan Slabbert, who was already the richest man in the whole of the Northern Transvaal, that would get all worked up over the prospect of unearthing buried treasure.

'Jan Slabbert has given Hendrik Buys a contract,' Neels Erasmus, the ouderling said. 'I learnt about it when I went there in connection with something of an ecclesiastical nature that happened at the Nagmaal before last. They will split whatever treasure they find. Jan Slabbert will get two-thirds and Hendrik Buys one-third.'

We said that it sounded a sinful arrangement, somehow. We also spoke much about what it said in the Good Book about treasures in heaven that the moth could not corrupt. That was after Neels Erasmus had said that there was no chance of the treasure having been buried on some neighbour's farm, instead, by mistake.

'Actually, according to the map,' the ouderling said, 'it would appear that the treasure is buried right in the middle of Jan Slabbert's farm, somewhere. Just about where his house is.'

'If Hendrik Buys has got any sense,' Jurie Bekker said, 'he would drive a tunnel right under Jan Slabbert's house, and as far as under his bedroom. If the tunnel came out under Jan Slabbert's bed, where he keeps that iron chest of his – well, even if Hendrik Buys is allowed to take only one-third of what is in there, it will still be something.'

We then said that perhaps that was the treasure that was marked on Hendrik Buys's map with a cross, but that they hadn't guessed it yet.

That gave me an idea. I asked how Jan Slabbert's daughter, Susannah, was taking all those irregular carryings-on on the farm. The ouderling moved the winking muscle of his left eye in a peculiar way.

'The moment Hendrik Buys came into the house I understood it all clearly,' he said, 'Susannah's face got all lit up as she kind of skipped into the kitchen to make fresh coffee. But Hendrik Buys was too wrapped up in the treasure-hunt business to notice, even. What a pity – a nice girl like that, and all.'

It seemed that that well-behaved young fellow, Andries Prinsloo, who always took the same place in the corner, was getting more respect for our company than ever. Because, this time, when he slipped out of the post office – and it was just about at that moment, too – he appeared actually to be walking on tiptoe.

Well, I didn't come across Jan Slabbert and Hendrik Buys again until about the time when they had finally decided to abandon the search. They had quarrelled quite often, too, by then. They would be on quite friendly terms when they showed the kafirs where to start digging another hole. But by the time the hole was very wide, and about ten foot deep, in blue slate, they would start quarrelling.

The funny part of it all was that Hendrik Buys remained optimistic about the treasure right through, and he wouldn't have given up, either, if in the course of their last quarrel Jan Slabbert had not decided the matter for him, bundling him on to the government lorry back to Zeerust, after kicking him.

The quarrel had to do with a hole eighteen foot deep, in gneiss.

But on that last occasion on which I saw them together in the voorkamer, Jan Slabbert and his daughter, Susannah, and Hendrik Buys, it seemed to me that Hendrik Buys was still very hopeful.

'There are lots of parts of the farm that I haven't crawled through yet,' Hendrik Buys explained. 'Likely places, according to the map, such as the pigsty. I have not yet crept through the pigsty. I must remember that for tomorrow. You see, the men who buried the treasure crept for the last part of the way through the bush in the dark.' Hendrik Buys paused. It was clear that an idea had struck him. 'Do you think it possible,' he asked, excitedly, 'that they might have crawled through the bush backwards – you know, in the dark? That is something that I had not thought of until this moment. What do you say, Oom Jan, tomorrow you and I go and creep backwards, in the direction of the pigsty?'

Jan Slabbert did not answer. And Susannah's efforts at keeping the conversation going made the situation seem all the more awkward. I felt sorry for her. It was a relief to us all when Neels Erasmus, the ouderling, arrived at the front door just then. He had come to see Jan Slabbert in connection with something of an apostolic description that might happen at the forthcoming Nagmaal.

I never saw Hendrik Buys again, but I did think of him quite a number of times afterwards, particularly on the occasion of Susannah Slabbert's wedding. And I wondered, in the course of his treasure-hunting, how much Hendrik Buys had possibly let slip through his fingers like sand. That was when the ceremony was over, and a couple of men among the wedding-guests were discharging their Mausers into the air – welcoming the bride as she was being lifted down from the Cape-cart by the quiet-mannered young fellow, Andries Prinsloo. He seemed more subdued than ever, now, as a bridegroom.

And so I understood then about the distracted air which Andries Prinsloo had worn throughout that feverish time of the great bushveld treasure-hunt; that it was in reality the half-dazed look of a man who had unearthed a pot of gold at the foot of the rainbow.

The Recognising Blues

I was ambling down Eloff Street, barefooted and in my shirt-sleeves, and with the recognising blues.

I had been smoking dagga, good dagga, the real rooibaard, with heads about a foot long, and not just the stuff that most dealers supply you with, and that is not much better than grass. When you smoke good dagga you get blue in quite a number of ways. The most common way is the frightened blues, when you imagine that your heart is palpitating, and that you can't breathe, and that you are going to die. Another form that the effect of dagga takes is that you get the suspicious blues, and then you imagine that all the people around you, your best friends and your parents included, are conspiring against you, so that when your mother asks you, 'How are you?' every word she says sounds very sinister, as though she knows that you have been smoking dagga, and that you are blue, and you feel that she is like a witch. The most innocent remark any person makes when you have got the suspicious blues seems to be impregnated with a whole world of underhand meaning and dreadful insinuation.

And perhaps you are right to feel this way about it. Is not the most harmless conversation between several human beings charged with the most diabolical kind of subterranean cunning, each person fortifying himself behind barbed-wire defences? Look at that painting of Daumier's, called Conversation Piece, and you will see that the two men and the woman concerned in this little friendly chat are all three of them taking part in a cloven-hoofed rite. You can see each one has got the suspicious blues.

There is also the once-over blues and a considerable variety of other kinds of blues. But the recognising blues doesn't come very often, and then it is only after you have been smoking the best kind of rooibaard boom, with ears that long.

When you have got the recognising blues you think you

know everybody you meet. And you go up and shake hands with every person that you come across, because you think you recognise him, and you are very glad to have run into him: in this respect the recognising blues is just the opposite of the suspicious blues.

A friend of mine, Charlie, who has smoked dagga for thirty years, says that he once had the recognising blues very bad when he was strolling through the centre of the town. And after he had shaken hands with lots of people who didn't know him at all, and whom he didn't know either, but whom he *thought* he knew, because he had the recognising blues – then a very singular thing happened to my friend, Rooker Charlie. For he looked in the display window of a men's outfitters, and he saw two dummies standing there, in the window, two dummies dressed in a smart line of gents' suitings, and with the recognising blues strong on him, Charlie thought that he knew those two dummies, and he thought that the one dummy was Max Chaitz, who kept a restaurant in Cape Town, and that the other dummy was a well-known snooker-player called Pat O'Callaghan.

And my friend Rooker Charlie couldn't understand how Max Chaitz and Pat O'Callaghan should come to be standing there holding animated converse in that shop-window. He didn't know, until that moment, that Max Chaitz and Pat O'Callaghan were even acquainted. But the sight of these two men standing there talking like that shook my friend Rooker Charlie up pretty badly. So he went home to bed. But early next morning he dashed round again to that men's outfitters, and then he saw that those two figures weren't Max Chaitz and Pat O'Callaghan at all, but two dummies stuck in the window. And he saw then that they didn't look even a bit like the two men he thought they were – especially the dummy that he thought was Max Chaitz. Because Max Chaitz is very short and fat, with a red, cross-looking sort of a face that you can't mistake in a million. Whereas the dummy was tall and slender and good-looking.

That was the worst experience that my friend Rooker Charlie ever had of the recognising blues.

And when I was taking a stroll down Eloff Street, that

evening, and I was barefooted and in my shirt-sleeves, then I also had a bad attack of the recognising blues. But it was the recognising blues in a slightly different form. I would first make up a name in my brain, a name that sounded good to me, and that I thought had the right sort of a rhythm to it. And then the first person I would see, I would think that he was the man whose name I had just thought out. And I would go up and address him by this name, and shake hands with him, and tell him how glad I was to see him.

And a name I thought up that sounded very fine to me, and impressive, with just the right kind of ring to it, was the name Sir Lionel Ostrich de Frontignac. It was a very magnificent name.

And so I went up, barefooted and in my shirt-sleeves, to the first man I saw in the street, after I had coined this name, and I took him by the hand, and I said, 'Well met, Sir Lionel. It is many years since last we met, Sir Lionel Ostrich de Frontignac.'

And the remarkable coincidence was that the man whom I addressed in this way actually was Sir Lionel Ostrich de Frontignac. But on account of his taking me for a bum – through my being bare-footed and in my shirt-sleeves – he wouldn't acknowledge that he really was Sir Lionel and that I had recognised him dead to rights.

'You are mistaken,' Sir Lionel Ostrich de Frontignac said, moving away from me, 'You have got the recognising blues.'

Great Uncle Joris

For quite a number of Boers in the Transvaal bushveld the expedition against Majaja's tribe of Bechuanas – we called them the Platkop kafirs – was unlucky.

There was a young man with us on this expedition who did not finish a story that he started to tell of a bygone war. And for a good while afterwards the relations were considerably strained between the old-established Transvalers living in these parts and the Cape Boers who had trekked in more recently.

I can still remember all the activity that went on north of the Dwarsberge at that time, with veldkornets going from one farmhouse to another to recruit burghers for the expedition, and with provisions and ammunition having to be got together, and with new stories being told every day about how cheeky the Platkop kafirs were getting.

I must mention that about that time a number of Boers from the Cape had trekked into the Marico Bushveld. In the Drogedal area, indeed, the recently-arrived Cape Boers were almost as numerous as the Transvalers who had been settled here for a considerable while. At that time I, too, still regarded myself as a Cape Boer, since I had only a few years before quit the Schweizer-Reineke district for the Transvaal. When the veldkornet came to my farm on his recruiting tour, I volunteered my services immediately.

'Of course, we don't want everybody to go on commando,' the veldkornet said, studying me somewhat dubiously, after I had informed him that I was from the Cape, and that older relatives of mine had taken part in wars against the kafirs in the Eastern Province. 'We need some burghers to stay behind to help guard the farms. We can't leave all that to the women and children.'

The veldkornet seemed to have conceived an unreasonable prejudice against people whose forebears had fought against the Xhosas in the Eastern Province. But I assured him that I was very anxious to join, and so in the end he consented. 'A volunteer is, after all, worth more to a fighting force than a man who has to be commandeered against his will,' the veldkornet said, stroking his beard. 'Usually.'

A week later, on my arrival at the big camp by the Steenbokspruit, where the expedition against the Platkop kafirs was being assembled, I was agreeably surprised to find many old friend and acquaintances from the Cape Colony among the burghers on commando. There were also a large number of others, whom I then met for the first time, who were introduced to me as new immigrants from the Cape.

Indeed, among ourselves we spoke a good deal about this proud circumstance – about the fact that we Cape Boers actually outnumbered the Transvalers in this expedition against Majaja – and we were glad to think that in time of need we had not failed to come to the help of our new fatherland. For this reason the coolness that made itself felt as between Transvaler and Cape Boer, after the expedition was over, was all the more regrettable.

We remained camped for a good number of days beside the Steenbokspruit. During that time I became friendly with Frikkie van Blerk and Jan Bezuidenhout, who were also originally from the Cape. We craved excitement. And when we were seated around the camp-fire, talking of life in the Eastern Province, it was natural enough that we should find ourselves swopping stories of the adventures of our older relatives in the wars against the Xhosas. We were all three young, and so we spoke like veterans, forgetting that our knowledge of frontier fighting was based only on hearsay. Each of us was an authority on the best way of defeating a Xhosa impi without loss of life to anybody except the members of the impi. Frikkie van Blerk took the lead in this kind of talk, and I may say that he was peculiar in his manner of expressing himself, sometimes. Unfeeling, you might say. Anyway, as the night wore on, there were in the whole Transvaal, I am sure, no three young men less worried than we were about the different kinds of calamities that, in this uncertain world, could overtake a Xhosa impi.

'Are you married, Schalk?' Jan Bezuidenhout asked me, suddenly.

'No,' I replied, 'but Frikkie van Blerk is. Why do you ask?'

Jan Bezuidenhout sighed.

'It is all right for you,' he informed me. 'But I am also married. And it is for burghers like Frikkie van Blerk and myself that a war can become a most serious thing. Who is looking after your place while you are on commando, Frikkie?'

Frikkie van Blerk said that a friend and neighbour, Gideon Kotze, had made special arrangements with the veldkornet, whereby he was released from service with the commando on condition that he kept an eye on the farms within twenty-mile radius of his own.

'The thought that Gideon Kotze is looking after things, in that way, makes me feel much happier,' Frikkie van Blerk added. 'It is nice for me to know that my wife will not be quite alone all the time.'

'Gideon Kotze –' Jan Bezuidenhout repeated, and sighed again.

'What do you mean by that sigh?' Frikkie van Blerk demanded, quickly, a nasty tone seeming to creep into his voice.

'Oh, nothing,' Jan Bezuidenhout answered, 'oh, nothing at all.'

As he spoke he kicked at a log on the edge of the fire. The fine sparks rose up very high in the still air and got lost in the leaves of the thorntree overhead.

Frikkie van Blerk cleared his throat. 'For that matter,' he said in a meaningful way to Jan Bezuidenhout, 'you are also a married man. Who is looking after your farm – and your wife – while you are sitting here?'

Jan Bezuidenhout waited for several moments before he answered.

'Who?' he repeated. 'Who? Why, Gideon Kotze – also.'

This time when Jan Bezuidenhout sighed, Frikkie van Blerk joined in audibly. And I, who had nothing at all to do with any part of this situation, seeing that I was not married, found myself sighing as well. And this time it was Frikkie van Blerk who kicked the log by the side of the fire. The chunk of white wood, which had been hollowed out by the ants, fell into several pieces, sending up a fiery shower so high that, to us, looking up to follow their flight, the yellow sparks became for a few moments almost indistinguishable from the stars.

'It's all rotten,' Frikkie van Blerk said, taking another kick at the crumbling log, and missing.

'There's something in the Bible about something else being something like the sparks flying upwards,' Jan Bezuidenhout announced. His words sounded very solemn. They served as an introduction to the following story that he told us:

'It was during my grandfather's time,' Jan Bezuidenhout said. 'My great-uncle Joris, who had a farm near the Keiskama, had been commandeered to take the field in the Fifth Kafir War. Before setting out for the war, my great-uncle Joris arranged for a friend and neighbour to visit his farm regularly, in case his wife needed help. Well, as you know, there is no real danger in a war against kafirs –'

'Yes, we know that,' Frikkie van Blerk and I agreed simultaneously, to sound knowledgeable.

'I mean, there's no danger as long as you don't go so near that a kafir can reach you with an assegai,' Jan Bezuidenhout continued. 'And, of course, no white man is as uneducated as all that. But what happened to my great-uncle Joris was that his horse threw him. The commando was retreating just about then –'

'To reload,' Frikkie van Blerk and I both said, eager to show how well-acquainted we were with the strategy used in kafir wars.

'Yes,' Jan Bezuidenhout went on. 'To reload. And there was no time for the commando to stop for my great-uncle Joris. The last his comrades saw of him, he was crawling on his hands and knees towards an aardvark-hole. They did not know whether the Xhosas had seen him. Perhaps the commando had to ride back fast because –'

Jan Bezuidenhout did not finish his story. For, just then, a veldkornet came with orders from Commandant Pienaar. We had to put out the fire. We had not to make so much noise. We were to hold ourselves in readiness, in case the kafirs launched a night attack. The veldkornet also instructed Jan Bezuidenhout to get his gun and go on guard duty.

'There was never any nonsense like this in the Cape,' Frikkie van Blerk grumbled, 'when we were fighting the Xhosas. It seems the Transvalers don't know what a kafir war is.'

By this time Frikkie van Blerk had got to believe that he actually had taken part in the campaigns against the Xhosas.

I have mentioned that there were certain differences between the Transvaler and the Cape Boers. For one thing, we from the Cape had a lightness of heart which the Transvalers lacked – possibly (I thought at the time) because the stubborn Transvaal soil made the conditions of life more harsh for them. And the difference between the two sections was particularly noticeable on the following morning, when Commandant Pienaar, after having delivered a short speech about how it was our duty to bring book-learning and refinement to the Platkop kafirs, gave the order to advance. We who were from the Cape cheered lustily. The Transvalers were, as always, subdued. They turned pale, too, some of them. We rode on for the best part of an hour. Frikkie van Blerk, Jan Bezuidenhout and I found ourselves together in a small group on one flank of the commando.

'It's funny,' Jan Bezuidenhout said 'but I don't see any kafirs, anywhere, with assegais. It doesn't seem to be like it was against the Xhosas –'

He stopped abruptly. For we heard what sounded surprisingly like a shot. Afterwards we heard what sounded surprisingly like more shots.

'These Platkop Bechuanas are not like the Cape Xhosas,' I agreed, then, dismounting.

In no time the whole commando had dismounted. We sought cover in dongas and behind rocks from the fire of an enemy who had concealed himself better than we were doing.

'No, the Xhosas were not at all like this,' Frikkie van Blerk announced, tearing off a strip of shirt to bandage a place in his leg from which the blood flowed. 'Why didn't the Transvalers let us know it would be like this?'

It was an ambush. Things happened very quickly. It became only too clear to me why the Transvalers had not shared in our enthusiasm earlier on, when we had gone over the rise together, at a canter, through the yellow grass, singing. I was still reflecting on this circumstance, some time later, when our commando remounted and galloped away out of that whole part of the district. To reload, we said, years afterwards, to strangers who asked. The last we saw of Jan Bezuidenhout was after he had his horse shot down from under him. He was crawling on hands and knees in the direction of an aardvark-hole.

'Like grand-uncle, like nephew,' Frikkie van Blerk said, when we were discussing the affair some time later, back in camp beside the Steenbokspruit. Frikkie van Blerk's unfeeling sally was not well-received.

Thus ended the expedition against Majaja, that brought little honour to the commando that took part in it. There was not a burgher who retained any sort of a happy memory of the affair. And for a good while afterwards the relations were strained between Transvaler and Cape Boer in the Marico.

It was with a sense of bitterness that, some months later, I had occasion to call to mind that Gideon Kotze, the man appointed to look after the farms of the burghers on commando, was a Transvaler.

And when I saw Gideon Kotze sitting talking to Jan Bezuidenhout's widow, on the front stoep of their house, I wondered what the story was, about his grand-uncle Joris, that Jan Bezuidenhout had not been able to finish telling.

The Ferreira Millions

Marthinus Taljaard lived in a house that his grandfather had built on the slope of a koppie in the Dwarsberge (Oom Schalk Lourens said). It was a big, rambling house with more rooms than what Marthinus Taljaard needed for just his daughter, Rosina, and himself. Marthinus Taljaard was known as the richest man in the whole of the Dwarsberge. It was these two circumstances that led to the koppie around his house becoming hollowed out with tunnels like the nest of a white ant.

Only a man who, like Marthinus Taljaard, already had more possessions in cattle and money than he knew what to do with, would still want more. That was why he listened to the story that Giel Bothma came all the way from Johannesburg to tell him about the Ferreira millions.

Of course, any Marico farmer would have been interested to hear what a young man in city clothes had to say, talking fast, about the meaning of a piece of yellow paper with lines and words on it, that he held in his hand. If Giel Bothma had come to me in that way, I would have listened to him, also. We would have sat on the stoep, drinking coffee. And I would have told him that it was a good story. I would also have shown him, if he was a young man willing to learn, how he could improve on it. Furthermore, I would have told him a few stories of my own, by way of guidance to him as to how to tell a story.

But towards milking time I would have to leave that young man sitting on the stoep, the while I went out to see what was happening in the cattle-kraal.

That was where Marthinus Taljaard, because he was the wealthiest man in die Dwarsberge, was different. He listened to Giel Bothma's story about the Ferreira millions from the early part of the forenoon onwards. He listened with his mouth open. And when it came to milking time, he invited Giel Bothma over to the kraal with him, with Giel Bothma still talking. And when it came to the time for feeding the pigs,

Giel Bothma helped to carry a heavy bucket of swill to the troughs, without seeming to notice the looks of surprise on the faces of the Bechuana farm labourers.

A little later, when Giel Bothma saw what the leaking bucket of swill had done to the legs of his smoothly-pressed trousers, he spoke a lot more. And what he used were not just all city words, either.

Anyway, the result of Giel Bothma's visit from Johannesburg was that he convinced Marthinus Taljaard, by means of the words and lines on that bit of yellow paper, that the Ferreira millions, a treasure comprised of gold and diamonds and elephant tusks, was buried on his farm.

We in the Marico had, needless to say, never heard of the Ferreira millions before. We knew only that Ferreira was a good Afrikaner name. And we often sang that old song, 'Vat jou goed en trek, Ferreira' – meaning to journey northwards out of the Cape to get away from English rule. Moreover, there was the Hans Ferreira family. They were Doppers and lived near Enzelsberg. But when you saw Hans Ferreira at the Indian store at Ramoutsa, lifting a few sheep-skins out of his donkey-cart and trying to exchange them for coffee and sugar, then you could not help greeting with a certain measure of amusement the idea conveyed by the words 'Ferreira millions'.

These were the matters that we discussed one midday while we were sitting around in Jurie Steyn's post office, waiting for our letters from Zeerust.

Marthinus Taljaard and his daughter, Rosina, had come to the post office, leaving Giel Bothma alone on the farm to work out, with the help of his yellowed map and the kafirs, the place where to dig the tunnel.

'This map with the Ferreira millions in gold and diamonds and elephant tusks,' Marthinus Taljaard said, pompously, sitting forward on Jurie Steyn's riempiestoel, 'was made many years ago – before my grandfather's time, even. That's why it is so yellow. Giel Bothma got hold of it just by accident. And the map shows clearly that the Portuguese explorer, Ferreira, buried his treasure somewhere in that koppie in the middle of my farm.'

'Anyway, that piece of paper is yellow enough,' Jurie Steyn said with a slight sneer. 'That paper is yellower than the iron pyrites that a prospector found at Witfontein so it must be gold, all right. And I can also see that it is gold, from the way you hang on to it.'

Several of us laughed, then.

'But I can't imagine there being such a thing as the Ferreira millions,' Stephanus van Tonder said, expressing what we all felt. 'Not if you think that Hans Ferreira's wife went to the last Nagmaal with a mimosa thorn holding up her skirt because they didn't have a safety-pin in the house.'

Marthinus Taljaard explained to us where we were wrong.

'The treasure was buried on my farm very long ago,' Marthinus Taljaard said, 'long before there were any white people in the Transvaal. It was the treasure that the Portuguese explorer, Ferreira, stole from the Mtosas. Maybe that Portuguese explorer was the ancestor of Hans Ferreira. I don't know. But I am talking about very long ago, before the Ferreiras were Afrikaners, but were just Portuguese. I am talking of *very* long ago.'

We told Marthinus Taljaard that he had better not make wild statements like that in Hans Ferreira's hearing. Hans Ferreira was a Dopper and quick-tempered. And even though he had to trade sheepskins for coffee and sugar, we said, not being able to wait to change the skins into money first, he would nevertheless go many miles out of his way with a sjambok to look for a man who spoke of him as a Portuguese.

And no matter how long ago either, we added.

Marthinus Taljaard sat up even straighter on the riempiestoel then.

By way of changing the conversation, Jurie Steyn asked Marthinus how he knew for certain that it was his farm on which the treasure was buried.

Marthinus Taljaard said that that part of the map was very clear.

'The site of the treasure, marked with a cross, is twelve thousand Cape feet north of Abjaterskop, in a straight line,' he said, 'so that's almost in the exact middle of my farm.'

He went on to explain, wistfully, that that was about the only part of the map that was in a straight line.

'It's all in Cape roods and Cape ells, like it has on the back of the school exercise books,' Marthinus Taljaard's daughter, Rosina, went on to tell us. "That's what makes it so hard for Mr. Bothma to work out the Ferreira map. We sometimes sit up to quite late at night, working out sums.'

After Marthinus Taljaard and Rosina had left, we said that young Giel Bothma must be pretty slow for a young man. Sitting up late at night with an attractive girl like Rosina Taljaard, and being able to think of nothing better to do than working out sums.

We also said it was funny that that first Ferreira should have filled up his treasure map with Cape measurements, when the later Ferreiras were in so much of a hurry to trek away from anything that even looked like the Cape.

In the months that followed there was a great deal of activity on Marthinus Taljaard's farm. I didn't go over there myself, but other farmers had passed that way, driving slowly in their mule-carts down the government road and trying to see all they could without appearing inquisitive. From them I learnt that a large number of tunnels had been dug into the side of a hill on which the Taljaard farm-house stood.

During those months, also, several of Marthinus Taljaard's Bechuanas left him and came to work for me. That new kind of work on Baas Taljaard's farm was too hard, one of them told me, brushing red soil off his elbow. He also said that Baas Taljaard was unappreciative of their best efforts at digging holes into the side of the koppie. And each time a hole came to an end, and there was no gold in it, or diamonds or elephant teeth, then Baas Taljaard would take a kick at whatever native was nearest.

'He kicked me as though it was my fault that there was no gold there,' another Bechuana said to me with a grin, 'instead of blaming it on that yellow paper with the writing on it.'

The Bechuana said that on a subsequent occasion, when there was no gold at the end of a tunnel that was particularly wide and long, Marthinus Taljaard ran a few yards (Cape yards, I suppose), and took a kick at Giel Bothma.

No doubt Baas Taljaard did that by mistake, the Bechuana

added, his grin almost as wide as one of those tunnels.

More months passed before I again saw Marthinus Taljaard and his daughter in Jurie Steyn's post office. Marthinus was saying that they were now digging a tunnel that he was sure was the right one.

'It points straight at my house,' he said, 'and where it comes up, there we'll find the treasure. We have now worked out from the map that the tunnel should go up, at the end. This wasn't clear before, because there is something missing –'.

'Yes, the treasure,' Jurie Steyn said, winking at Stephanus van Tonder.

'No,' Rosina interjected, flushing. 'There is a corner missing from the map. That bit of the map remained between the thumb and forefinger of the man in the bar when he gave it to Giel Bothma.'

'We only found out afterwards that Giel Bothma had that map given to him by crooks in a bar,' Marthinus Taljaard said. 'If I had known about that at the start, I don't know if I would have been so keen about it. Why I listened was because Giel Bothma was so well-dressed, in city clothes, and all.'

Marthinus Taljaard stirred his coffee.

'But he isn't any more,' he resumed, reflectively. 'Not well-dressed, I mean. You should have seen how his suit looked after the first week of tunnelling.'

We had quite a lot to say after Marthinus Taljaard and Rosina left.

'Crooks in a bar,' Stephanus van Tonder snorted. 'It's all clear to me, now. That tunnel is going to come up right under Marthinus Taljaard's bed, where he keeps his money in that tamboetie chest. I am sure that map has got nothing to do with the Ferreira treasure at all. But it seems a pretty good map of the Taljaard treasure.'

We also said that it was a very peculiar way that that crook had of *giving* Giel Bothma the map. With one corner of it remaining in his hand. It certainly looked as though Giel Bothma must have pulled on it, a little.

We never found out how much truth there was in our speculation. For we learnt some time later that Giel Bothma did get hold of the Taljaard fortune, after all. He got it by marrying Rosina. And that last tunnel did come up under a part of Marthinus Taljaard's rambling old house, built on the side of the koppie. It came up right in front of the door of Rosina Taljaard's bedroom.

The Missionary

That kafir carving hanging on the wall of my voorkamer, (Oom Schalk Lourens said), it's been there many years. It was found in the loft of the pastorie at Ramoutsa after the death of the Dutch Reformed missionary there, Reverend Keet.

To look at, it's just one of those figures that a kafir woodcarver cuts out of soft wood, like ndubu or mesetla. But because I know him quite well, I can still see a rough sort of resemblance to Reverend Keet in that carving, even though it is now discoloured with age and the white ants have eaten away parts of it. I first saw this figure in the study of the pastorie at Ramoutsa when I went to call on Reverend Keet. And when, after his death, the carving was found in the loft of the pastorie, I brought it here. I kept it in memory of a man who had strange ideas about what he was pleased to call Darkest Africa.

Reverend Keet had not been at Ramoutsa very long. Before that he had worked at a mission station in the Cape. But, as he told us, ever since he had paid a visit to the Marico district, some years before, he had wanted to come to the Northern Transvaal. He said he had obtained, in the bushveld along the Malopo River, a feeling that here was the real Africa. He said there was a spirit of evil in these parts that he believed it was his mission to overcome.

We who had lived in the Marico for the greater part of our lives wondered what we had done to him.

On his previous visit here Reverend Keet had stayed long enough to meet Elsiba Grobler, the daughter of Thys Grobler of Drogedal. Afterwards he sent for Elsiba to come down to the Cape to be his bride.

And so we thought that the missionary had remembered with affection the scenes that were the setting for his courtship. And that was why he came back here. So you can imagine how disappointed we were in learning the truth.

Nevertheless, I found it interesting to listen to him, just because he had such outlandish views. And so I called on him quite regularly when I passed the mission station on my way back from the Indian store at Ramoutsa.

Reverend Keet and I used to sit in his study, where the curtains were half-drawn, as they were in the whole pastorie. I supposed it was to keep out the bright sunshine that Darkest Africa is so full of.

'Only yesterday a kafir child hurt his leg falling out of a withaak tree,' Reverend Keet said to me on one occasion. 'And the parents didn't bring the child here so that Elsiba or I could bandage him up. Instead, they said there was a devil in the withaak. And so they got the witch-doctor to fasten a piece of crocodile skin to the child's leg, to drive away the devil.'

So I said that just showed you how ignorant a kafir was. They should have fastened the crocodile skin to the withaak, instead, like the old people used to do. That would drive the devil away quick enough, I said.

Reverend Keet did not answer. He just shook his head and looked at me in a pitying sort of way, so that I felt sorry I had spoken.

To change the subject I pointed to a kafir wood-carving standing on a table in the corner of the study. That same wood-carving you see today hanging on the wall of my voorkamer.

'Here's now something that we want to encourage,' Reverend Keet said in answer to my question. 'Through art perhaps we can bring enlightenment to these parts. The kafirs here seem to have a natural talent for wood-carving. I have asked Willem Terreblanche to write to the education department for a text-book on the subject. It will be another craft that we can teach to the children at the school.'

Willem Terreblanche was the assistant teacher at the mission station.

'Anyway, it will be more useful than that last text-book we got on how to make paper serviettes with tassels,' Reverend Keet went on, half to himself. Then it was a though an idea struck him. 'Oh, by the way,' he asked, 'would you perhaps like, say, a few dozen paper serviettes with tassels to take home with you?'

I declined his offer in some haste.

Reverend Keet started talking about that carving again.

'You wouldn't think it was meant for me, now, would you?' he asked.

And because I am always polite, that way, I said no, certainly not.

'I mean, just look at the top of my body,' he said. 'It's like a sack of potatoes. Does the top part of *my* body look like a sack of potatoes?'

And once again I said no, oh no.

Reverend Keet laughed, then – rather loudly, I thought – at the idea of that wood-carver's ignorance. I laughed quite loudly, also, to make it clear that I, too, thought that that kafir wood-carver was very ignorant.

'All the same, for a raw kafir who has had no training,' the missionary continued, 'it's not bad. But take that self-satisfied sort of smile, now, that he put on my face. It only came out that way because the kafir who made the carving lacks the skill to carve my features as they really are. He hasn't got technique.'

I thought, well, maybe that ignorant Bechuana didn't know any more what technique was than I did. But I did think he had a pretty shrewd idea how to carve a wooden figure of Reverend Keet.

'If a kafir had the impudence to make a likeness like that of me, with such big ears and all,' I said to Reverend Keet, 'I would kick him in the ribs. I would kick him for being so ignorant, I mean.'

It was then that Elsiba brought us in our coffee. Although she was now the missionary's wife, I still thought of her as Elsiba, a bushveld girl whom I had seen grow up.

'You've still got that thing there,' Elsiba said to her husband, after she had greeted me. 'I won't have you making a fool of yourself. Every visitor to the pastorie who sees this carving goes away laughing at you.'

'They laugh at the kafir who made it, Elsiba, because of his poor technique,' Reverend Keet said, drawing himself up in his chair.

'Anyway, I'm taking it out of here,' Elsiba answered.

I have since then often thought of that scene. Of the way Elsiba Keet walked from the room, with the carving standing upright on the tray that she had carried the coffee-cups on. Because of its big feet that wooden figure did not fall over when Elsiba flounced out with the tray. And in its stiff, wooden bearing the figure seemed to be expressing the same disdain of the kafir wood-carver's technique as what Reverend Keet had.

I remained in the study a long time. And all the while the missionary talked of the spirit of evil that hung over the Marico like a heavy blanket. It was something brooding and oppressive, he said, and it did something to the souls of men. He asked me whether I hadn't noticed it myself.

So I told him that I had. I said that he had taken the very words out of my mouth. And I proceeded to tell him about the time Jurie Bekker had impounded some of my cattle that he claimed had strayed into his mealie lands.

'You should have seen Jurie Bekker the morning that he drove off my cattle along the government road,' I said. 'An evil blanket hung over him, all right. You could almost see it. A striped kafir blanket.'

I also told the missionary about the sinful way in which Niklaas Prinsloo had filled in those compensation forms for losses which he had never suffered, even. And about the time Gert Haasbroek sold me what he said was a pedigree Afrikander bull, and that was just an animal he had smuggled through from the Protectorate one night, with a whole herd of other beasts, and that died afterwards of grass-belly.

I said that the whole of the Marico district was just bristling with evil, and I could give him many more examples, if he would care to listen.

But Reverend Keet said that was not what he meant. He said he was talking of the unnatural influences that hovered over this part of the country. He had felt those things particularly at the swamps by the Malopo, he said, with the green bubbles coming up out of the mud and with those trees that were like shapes oppressing your mind when it is fevered. But it was like that everywhere in the bushveld, he said. With the sun pouring down at midday, for instance, and the whole veld very still, it was yet as though there was a high black wind, somewhere, an old lost wind. And he felt a chill in all his bones, he said, and it was something unearthly.

It was interesting for me to hear the Reverend Keet talk like that. I had heard the same sort of thing before from strangers. I wondered what he could take for it.

'Even here in this study, where I am sitting talking to you,' he added. 'I can sense a baleful influence. It is some form of – of something skulking, somehow.'

I knew, of course, that Reverend Keet was not making any underhanded allusion to my being there in his study. He was too religious to do a thing like that. Nevertheless, I felt uncomfortable. Shortly afterwards I left.

On my way back in the mule-cart I passed the mission school. and I thought then that it was funny that Elsiba was so concerned that a kafir should not make a fool of her husband with a wood-carving of him. Because she did not seem to mind making a fool of him in another way. From the mule-cart I saw Elsiba and Willem Terreblanche in the doorway of the school-room. And from the way they were holding hands I could see they were not discussing paper serviettes with tassels, or any similar school subjects.

Still, as it turned out, it never came to any scandal in the district. For Willem Terreblanche left some time later to take up a teaching post in the Free State. And after Reverend Keet's death Elsiba allowed a respectable interval to elapse before she went to the Free State to marry Willem Terreblanche.

Some distance beyond the mission school I came across the Ramoutsa witch-doctor that Reverend Keet had spoken about. The witch-doctor was busy digging up roots on the veld for medicine. I reined in the mules and the witch-doctor came up to me. He had on a pair of brown leggings and a woman's corset. And he carried an umbrella. Around his neck he wore a few feet of light-green tree-snake that didn't look as though it had been dead very long. I could see that the witch-doctor was particular about how he dressed when he went out.

I spoke to him in Sechuana about Reverend Keet. I told him that Reverend Keet said the Marico was a bad place. I also told him that the missionary did not believe in the cure of fastening a piece of crocodile skin to the leg of a child who had fallen out of a withaak tree. And I said that he did not seem to think, either, that if you fastened crocodile skin to the withaak it would drive the devil out of it.

The witch-doctor stood thinking for some while. And when he spoke again it seemed to me that in his answer there was a measure of wisdom.

'The best thing,' he said 'would be to fasten a piece of crocodile skin on to the baas missionary.'

It seemed quite possible that the devils were not all just in the Marico bushveld. There might be one or two inside Reverend Keet himself, also.

Nevertheless, I have often since then thought of how almost inspired Reverend Keet was when he said that there was evil going on around him, right here in the Marico. In his very home – he could have said. With the curtains half-drawn and all. Only, of course, he didn't mean it that way.

Yet I have also wondered if, in the way that he did mean it – when he spoke of those darker things that he claimed were at work in Africa – I wonder if there, too, Reverend Keet was as wide off the mark as one might lightly suppose.

That thought first occurred to me after Reverend Keet's death and Elsiba's departure. In fact, it was when the new missonary took over the pastorie at Ramoutsa and this woodcarving was found in the loft.

But before I hung up the carving where you see it now, I first took the trouble to pluck off the lock of Reverend Keet's hair that had been glued to it. And I also plucked out the nails that had been driven – by Elsiba's hands, I could not but think – into the head and heart.

Rosser

There was one convict in the prison that I saw at intervals on parade. His name was Rosser. He was old and tall and dried-up. He was also very morose. He was doing time for murder. I never saw him speak to anybody. On exercise he always walked grim and toothless and alone. Other convicts told me about Rosser. He was doing a very long stretch for murder. Nobody seemed to know exactly how long. And it was doubtful whether even Rosser knew any more. With the years he had grown soft in the head, they said.

It was a peculiar sort of murder, too, that Rosser was doing time for, they explained. It appeared that, suspecting his wife of infidelity, he had murdered her on the Marico farm where they lived. And he had disposed of the body by burying it under the dung floor of the voorkamer of the house. So much was, perhaps, reasonable. He had murdered his wife, and the first place he could think of burying her was under the floor of the living-room.

He had filled in the hole again neatly and had smeared the floor with nice fresh cow-dung.

But what made the judge raise his eye-brows, rather, was when it was revealed in court that Rosser had held a dance in that same voorkamer on the evening of the very day on which he had performed those simple sacrificial and funeral rites – whereby his hands got twice stained.

There was a good attendance at that bushveld party, which went on a long time, and several of the dancers afterwards declared in court that they were very shocked when they learnt that they had been dancing all night on top of the late Mrs. Rosser's upturned face. It is true that a number of guests were able to salve their consciences to a limited degree with the reflection that they had danced only the simple country measures; they had not gone in for jazz. One girl also said in court, 'Oh, well, I just danced lightly.'

Nevertheless, the Rosser case provided the local dominee, who was a stern Calvinist, with first-class material on which to base a whole string of sermons against the evils of dancing . . .

The above, more or less, were the facts about Rosser's crime that I was able to glean from fellow-convicts. But there were several features that mystified me.

'But why did he do it?' I asked a blue-coat, 'I mean what did he want to go and throw party for – getting all those people to dance on top of his wife's dead body?'

'It's just because he's got no feelings,' the blue-coat said. 'That's what. Just look at the way his jaw sticks out without teeth in his head. No feelings, that's what.'

Another convict, again, would reply to the same question, 'Well, I suppose it was to get the floor stamped down again. They give dances in the bushveld just to stamp the ground down hard.'

A third convict would proffer the explanation, 'Well, he was damned glad his wife was dead, see?'

There was a distressing lack of uniformity about the answers I got. And then it suddenly struck me that the convicts were, of course, all going by hearsay. Because, when I questioned them on that point, individually, each agreed that he had never spoken to Rosser. Not as much as passed him the time of day, ever. Rosser just wasn't the sort of person you would ever take it into your head to talk to, anyway.

If Rosser's case was as horrifying as all that, I wondered, then why did the Governor-General-in-Council reprieve him? Why wasn't he hanged? That question, too, I once put to a fellow-convict. And the answer I got surprised me not a little.

'I suppose,' the convict said, 'why Rosser was reprieved was because the judge put in a recommendation for mercy – because it was such a good party.'

In the end, there was nothing else for me to do about it. I had to get the facts from Rosser himself, at first-hand. I had to approach him and talk to him, and put my question to him straight out. That wasn't an easy thing to do. I had to screw up every nerve in my body to get so far as to address him. It took me a little while to work up enough guts to go up to Rosser and say, 'Hallo. How do you do?' In fact, it took me about two years.

And when I did get so far as to talk to Rosser, I realised that he was quite harmless. Only, because nobody had spoken to him for so many years, it was with a considerable effort on his part that he was able to enunciate any words at all. And then, when he spoke, I had to turn my face aside. The way his jaw came up and the way his toothless gums got exposed when he struggled with the unfamiliar thing of speech – the sight of it gave me an acute sense of disgust. But, God knows, his story was simple enough.

'I done my wife in with a chopper because she was sweet on another man,' Rosser explained, 'and I buried her under the floor and all. And then what happens, but when I got everything clean again, a lot of people come in with concertinas and bottles of wine and brandy. It was a surprise party. And I couldn't say, "Look here, you can't hold a surprise party in my dining-room. I just buried my wife here." So I just said, "Welcome, friends. Come in and sing and dance".'

So there was no more to the whole thing than just that.

'And the man,' Rosser went on, in his lewd-gummed wrestling with the strangeness of words, 'the man that I thought my wife was sweet on – he was the one that got the neighbours together and said, "Let us go and have a surprise party at Rosser's place." And all that night he was looking for my wife. But I dunno . . .'

'Dunno what,' I asked with feigned interest, for I was anxious to be off. One conversation with Rosser in a life-time was enough.

'I dunno if my wife ever really was sweet on him,' Rosser said. 'I mean, now I been in prison fifteen years, I dunno. Because I have always been a much better-looking man that what that man is.'

The Murderess

'One of your best friends, wasn't he, Frans?' Japie Krige asked of me in the Gouspoort post office after I had read the letter. 'You knew them both well, didn't you?'

I nodded, recalling a time when there had been a similar letter in the post, but on *that* occasion not addressed to me. I now read the letter from Willem Lemmer's widow again:

Dear Frans,

You will no doubt be much grieved to learn that my husband is no more. During his last days he spoke of you often. Though he fought hard for life he seemed to know the end was coming. Some time before his death Willem said to me: 'Stoffelina, I would wish Frans to come here after I am gone that he may take for himself what he would like to have as a remembrance of me.'

I therefore write you of Willem's last wish that concerns you and say that I would be glad if you could come to the farm when you are able.

Stoffelina Lemmer

P.S. The funeral was on Friday. Elder Duvenhage read from the Gospel of Mark and we sang from Psalm 18 three verses and from Hymn 27 the first and last verses. The elder spoke very beautifully of Willem.

I could not but recall the time when I had seen a very similar letter, but held in another's hands.

'Not so very old, either, was he?' Japie Krige remarked when we left the post office together.

I said, no, but it was an unhealthy area, that low-lying stretch in the fold of the 'Nwati hills.

'If you ask me,' Japie Krige replied, 'the whole of the bush-veld seems pretty unhealthy. If it's not malaria, it's leopards or it's –'

Japie Krige was from the city. He and I were partners in a corundum proposition outside Gouspoort. And in spite of the way he talked sometimes, decrying the necessarily primitive conditions of our mode of existence, the fact remained that he had adapted himself remarkably well to a life which, if it was rough, nevertheless offered a physical freedom of which a city-dweller could know nothing – and bestowed on the spirit a quality not of breadth but of intensity. To the mind of one living in the bush, the bush did strange things. One's imaginative faculties could not but be stimulated.

'– or it's snakes,' Japie Krige went on. 'Well, that's unhealthy enough, if you ask me.'

Yet, in the main, with Japie Krige that sort of thing was just talk. And I suspected that if he were ever presented with the opportunity of establishing himself in the city again he would not take advantage of it. I felt that in spite of what he said, the bushveld had got into Japie Krige's blood and that he would not quit it readily.

We walked down the dusty road of the Bechuana village of Gouspoort – of which the post office next to the general store was the most important building – on the way back to our camp. It was early afternoon. The heat was oppressive. Vast numbers of goats were sprawled about the place – lying in the half-shade of thorn-scrub, pressing up against the wall of the mission station, seeking shelter from the sun on the cool side of low rocks that cast shadows no more than a few inches in length. The goats littered the village like crumpled pieces of newspaper.

We walked round a fat, tawny-coloured sow that lay with her large litter in the middle of the road.

'Are you going?' Japie Krige asked me. 'I could come with you. If you thought I wouldn't be in the way, that is.'

The silence of early afternoon lay over the village and over the veld. From a great distance there came the sound of a piccanin's voice – a herdboy calling his cattle. That sound seemed part of, and blended integrally with, the stillness.

'I don't know whether I should go,' I answered after an interval of thought. 'I really don't know.'

The sandy road before us shimmered in the heat. Fragments

of bottle glass on an anthill flung back the sun's rays with a brilliance as piercing as the edges of the shards themselves.

'I don't mean that you should go to *collect* anything,' Japie Krige went on, sounding half-apologetic. 'I am just thinking that – well, you know, when it's a case of somebody's death – the death of a close friend – well, you feel you want to do something, don't you? I don't suggest that you should go there just to fetch away his watch, say, as a keepsake.'

Japie Krige made that last remark, I knew, to give a sardonic twist to his words. Like many people with a true warmth of feeling he drew back from the idea of appearing sentimental.

I picked up a piece of rusted barbed wire and flung it a good distance into the veld. Lying where it was on the road, that barbed wire was a menace to the tyres of any motor vehicle passing that way. Not that the road was much used, of course, by any form of mechanical transport.

'Willem Lemmer did have a watch,' I said to Japie Krige, 'an old-fashioned gold watch with a chain and with an enamel painting on the case. The watch should be –'

It was a queer thing. Just on account of my having *thought* of a motor car in connection with that length of barbed wire the spell of the bushveld village's torpor seemed to be lifted from me. The certain knowledge that there *was* that outside world of civilisation and rush and power stations and materialistic progress and cigarette-ends lying on pavements – all this freed me for a while from a hypnotic power whose true nature I understood only too well and from whose horror I recoiled almost as unthinkingly as I yielded to its fascination. For the feelings that went with a walk along the road through a bushveld Bantu village on a hot afternoon formed, I knew, a part of those other, darker feelings that held in them both lure and menace.

'– should be worth quite a good bit,' I said to Japie Krige.

'I hope there aren't any snakes here,' Japie Krige said as we stood with our suitcases on the tracks of the railway siding, and the train was slowly disappearing from view among the thorntrees.

Japie Krige surveyed, with marked disfavour, the tangled growths – varying in hue from a diversity of greys to livid greens – through which a footpath looked a good deal like a snake, too, I thought – like a brown mamba even, twisting its way through the grass. I did not, however, mention that to Japie Krige.

There was no one to meet us at the siding. For we had not written to Willem Lemmer's widow that we were coming. Still, the Lemmer farmhouse was not many miles distant. It was certainly fewer miles away than one would readily imagine, standing on the railway track and seeing to the east and west a low line of koppies that looked all the more desolate for their intermittent covering of bush and with northern and southern horizons hidden from view by the immediate trees.

'If they didn't have those koppies there,' Japie Krige said, unconsciously speaking as though he were in a city and the koppies were buildings erected by human agency, 'then it wouldn't feel quite so lonely. It would be bad enough, I mean. But if you had around you just bush then you could imagine that there is nothing but bush anywhere. But with koppies, there, you can *see* that there is in the whole world nothing but bush.'

Japie Krige did not sound very cheerful. He grew even more discouraged when I informed him that those koppies were the 'Nwatis. He remembered what I had told him about how unhealthy the area was. At the same time I said to him that if he was really afraid of snakes we could quit the footpath and take the wagon-road to the Lemmer farm instead. Only it was a longer way round. But Japie said no, we could stick to the footpath.

He said he felt there were worse things in the folds of the 'Nwati hills than snakes. I did not think it necessary to tell him how right he was.

What was singular about my own feelings, I found, was that having once decided to come there the misgivings that obsessed my mind during that afternoon walk through the African village of Gouspoort were suddenly dissipated. Even though there was now no more turning back I felt almost buoyant – even though the way I had to tread was now narrowed to a footpath.

And the fact was that I was not now much concerned with how I felt about things. I was far more interested in Japie Krige's reactions. I could not help but reflect how much they had in common with my own feelings of a former time when I had carried a suitcase down that winding footpath in the company of a man who had a letter that was similar to the letter folded in my breast pocket.

For some distance the way skirted a barbed wire fence. On one hand was the bush, on the other the stubble of mealie land.

I drew Japie Krige's attention to this circumstance.

'That's one thing about Willem Lemmer's widow,' I said to Japie. 'She doesn't let tragedy overwhelm her. You can see she's got things on this farm in hand all right. You'd think that with the boss dead the Bantu would be taking it easy sitting in front of their huts drinking beer. Or lying by a stream smoking dagga. But from the quick way they are a-moving this way and that you'd never think that their master is in the cold, cold ground.'

Japie Krige looked at me in surprise.

'You know, Frans,' he said, 'the way you're talking it seems as though you've got no feelings about death.'

I replied, trying to sound cryptic, that some day, some day, perhaps, he would find out, 'Only in that case,' I added, 'it will be after my time.'

It was only when the footpath came to an end and we emerged into the homestead clearing with the farmhouse at the end of it that my former trepidation returned. The day was almost over. From the kraal came shouted words and the clanking of milk-pails. I looked down. At my feet a belated ant was scurrying home from work. I found that I was noticing trivial things again. Once more my spirit was obsessed with a fear whose cause I knew but whose nature I could not define for it was a mixed emotion. Inextricably blended with terror was something that came near to exaltation – but it was exaltation of an unholy sort.

And it was then that Japie Krige took it into his head to become facetious. I attributed his change of mood to the relief occasioned in his mind by the sight, in the distance, of a farmhouse with smoke rising from the chimney, suggesting comfort and human cheer after a journey through miles of inhospitable bush. Another thing too, I thought, was that Japie Krige was seeking to imitate my own somewhat unhappy attempt at a *plaisanterie* of earlier on. Only, when I spoke like that, I said to myself, it was still daylight.

'Not a bad-looking place,' was what Japie Krige said. 'Why don't you marry Willem Lemmer's widow? After all, you've come here for something to remind you of him. Well, his widow's something he's left behind.'

It was on the tip of my tongue to ask Japie Krige why *he* didn't marry her. But I refrained. Perhaps he would yet, one day. After all, the African bush *was* getting into his blood.

By now it was quite dark. But the gloom could not entirely shroud a fenced-in area to our right in which there were mounds. Not all of the mounds had headstones.

A dove cooed.

Some small creature of the night stirred in the dark green near us.

It seemed to me that my voice sounded exactly as Willem Lemmer's voice had sounded on that first occasion on which he and I had come together to the front door. And now, I used the same words that Willem Lemmer spoke then.

'I got your letter,' I said to Stoffelina as she opened the door for us.

I saw at once that she looked more beautiful than ever.

The Question

Stefanus Malherbe had difficulty in getting access to the President, to put to him the question of which we were all anxious to learn the answer.

It was at Waterval Onder and President Kruger was making preparations to leave for Europe to enlist the help of foreign countries in the Transvaal's struggle against England. General Louis Botha had just been defeated at Dalmanutha. Accordingly, we who were the last of the Boer commandos in the field, found ourselves hemmed in against the Portuguese border by the British forces, the few miles of railway line from Nelspruit to Komatipoort being all that still remained to us of Transvaal soil. The Boer War had hardly begun and it already looked like the end.

But when we had occasion to watch from a considerable distance a column of British dragoons advancing through a half-mile stretch of bush country, there were those of us who realised that the Boer War might, after all, not be over yet. It took the column two hours to get through that bush.

Although we who served under Veld-kornet Stefanus Malherbe were appointed to the duty of guarding President Kruger during those last days, we had neither the opportunity nor the temerity to talk to him in that house at Waterval Onder. For one thing, there were those men with big stomachs and heavy gold watch-chains all crowding around the President with papers they wanted him to sign. Nevertheless when the news came that the English had broken through at Dalmanutha we overheard some of those men say, not raising their voices unduly, that something or other was no longer worth the paper it was written on. Next morning, when President Kruger again came on the front stoep of the house, alone this time, we were for the first time able to see him clearly instead of through the thick screen of grey smoke being blown into his face from imported cigars.

'Well,' Thys Haasbroek said, 'I hope the President when he gets to Europe enlists the right kind of foreigners to come and fight for the Republic. It would be too bad if he came back with another crowd of *uitlanders* with big stomachs and watch-chains, waving papers for concessions.'

I mention this remark made by one of the burghers at Waterval Onder with the President to show you that there was not a uniform spirit of bitter-end loyalty animating the three thousand men who saw day by day the net of the enemy getting more tightly drawn around them. Indeed, speaking for myself, I must confess that the enthusiasm of those of our leaders who at intervals addressed us, exhorting us to courage, had but a restricted influence on my mind.

Especially when the orders came for the rolling stock to be dynamited.

For we had brought with us, in our retreat from Magersfontein, practically all the carriages and engines and trucks of the Transvaal and Orange Free State railways. At first we were much saddened by the necessity for destroying the property of our country. But afterwards something got into our blood which made it all seem like a good joke. I know that our own little group that was under the leadership of Veld-kornet Stefanus Malherbe really derived a considerable amount of enjoyment, towards the end, out of blowing railway engines and whole trains into the air. A couple of former shunters who were on commando with us would say things like, 'There goes the Cape Mail via Fourteen Streams,' and we would fling ourselves into a ditch to escape the flying fragments of wood and steel. One of them also used to shout, 'All seats for Bloemfontein,' or 'First stop Elandsfontein,' after the fuse was lit and he would blow his whistle and wave a green flag. For several days it seemed that between Nelspruit and Hectorspruit you couldn't look up at any part of the sky without seeing wheels in it.

And during all this time we treated the whole affair as fun and the former shunters had got to calling out, 'There goes the nine-twenty to De Aar,' against the signals and, 'There's a girl with fair hair travelling by herself in the end compartment.' Being railwaymen, they couldn't think of anything else to say.

Because the war of the big commandos, and of men like Generals Joubert and Cronje, was over it seemed to us that all the fighting was just about done. We did not know that the Boer War of General de Wet and Ben Viljoen and General Muller was then only about to begin.

The next order that our veld-kornet, Stefanus Malherbe, brought us from the commandant was for the destruction of our stores and field guns and ammunition dumps as well. All we had to retain were our Mausers and horses, the order said. That did not give us much cause for hope. At the same time the first of General Louis Botha's burghers from the Dalmanutha fight began to arrive in our camp. They were worn out from their long retreat and many of them had acquired the singular habit of looking round over their shoulder very quickly, every so often, right in the middle of a conversation. Their presence did not help to inspire us with military ardour. One of these burghers was very upset at our having blown up all the trains. He had been born and bred in the *gramadoelas* and had been looking forward to his first journey by rail.

'I just wanted to feel how the thing rides,' he said in disappointed tones, in between trying to wipe off stray patches of yellow lyddite stains he had got at Dalmanutha. 'But even if there *was* still another train left I suppose it would be too late, now.'

'Yes, I am sure it would be too late,' I said, also looking quickly over my shoulder. There was something infectious about this habit that Louis Botha's burghers had brought with them.

Actually, of course, it was not yet too late for there was still a train, with the engine and carriages intact, waiting to take the President out of the Transvaal into Portuguese territory. There were also in the Boer ranks men whose loyalty to the Republic never wavered even in the darkest times. It had been a very long retreat from the Northern Cape Province through the Orange Free State and the Transvaal to where we were now shut in near the Komati River. And it had all happened so quickly.

The Boer withdrawal, when once it got under way, had

been fast and complete. I found it not a little disconcerting to think that on one day I had seen the President seated in a spider just outside Paardeberg drinking buttermilk and then on another day, only a few months later, I had seen him sitting on the front stoep of a house at Waterval Onder a thousand miles away, drinking brandy. Moreover, he was getting ready to move again.

'If it is only to Europe that he is going, then it is not so bad,' said an old farmer with a long beard who was an ignorant man in many ways, but whose faith had not faltered throughout the retreat. 'I would not have liked our beloved President to have to travel all that way back to the Northern Cape where we started from. He hasn't the strength for so long a journey. I am glad that it is only to Russia that he is going.'

Because he was not demoralised by defeat, as so many of us were, we who listened to this old farmer's words were touched by his simple loyalty. Indeed the example set by men of his sort had a far greater influence on the course of the war during the difficult period ahead than the speeches that our leaders came round and made to us from time to time.

Certainly we did not feel that the veld-kornet, Stefanus Malherbe, was a tower of strength. We did not dislike him nor did we distrust him. We only felt, after a peculiar fashion, that he was too much like the same kind of man that we ourselves were. So we did not have over-much respect for him.

I have said that we ordinary burghers did not have the temerity to approach the President and to talk to him as man to man of the matter that we wanted to know about. And so we hung back a little while Stefanus Malherbe, an officer on whom many weighty responsibilities reposed, put out his chest and strode toward the house to interview the President. 'Put out your stomach,' one of the burghers called out. He was of course thinking of those men who lately had surrounded the President with their papers and watch-chains and cigars.

And then, when Stefanus Malherbe was moving in the direction of the *voorkamer* where we knew the President to be, and when the rest of the members of our *veldkornetskap* had drawn itself together in a little knot that stood nervously waiting just off the stoep for the President's reply – I suppose it had to happen that just then a newly-appointed general should have decided to treat us to a patriotic talk. Under other circumstances we would have been impressed perhaps, but at the point of time, when we had already blown up our trains and stores and ammunition dumps, and had sunk the pieces that remained of the Staat's Artillerie in the Komati River – along with some paper we had captured in earlier battle – we were not an ideal audience.

We stood still, out of politeness, and listened. But all the time we were wondering if the veld-kornet would perhaps be able to slip away at the end of the speech and manage to get in a few words with President Kruger after all. Anyway I am sure that we took in very little of what the newly appointed general had to say.

In the end the general realised the position too. We gathered that he had known he was going to get the appointment that day and that he had prepared a speech for the occasion, to deliver before the President and the State Council, but that he had been unable to have his say in the house because of the bustle attendant upon the President's impending departure. Consequently the general delivered his set speech to us, the first group of burghers he encountered on his way out. After he had got us to sing Psalm 83 and had adjured each one of us to humble himself before the Lord, the general explained at great length that if we could perhaps not hope for victory, since victory might be beyond our capacity, we could still hope for a more worthy kind of defeat.

We made no response to his eloquence. We did not sweep our hats upward in a cheer. We did not call out, '*Ou perd!*'. We were only concerned with the veld-kornet's chances of having a word with the President before it was too late. The general understood, eventually, that our hearts were not in his address and so he concluded his speech rather abruptly. 'Some defeats are greater than victories,' he said, and he paused for a little while to survey us before adding, 'but not this one, I think.'

The meeting having ended suddenly like that, Veldkornet Stefanus Malherbe did, after all, manage to get into the *voorkamer* to speak to President Kruger alone. That much we knew. But when he came out of the house, the veld-kornet was silent about his conversation with the president. He did not tell us what the President had said in answer to his question. And in the next advance of the English, which was made within that weekend and which took them right into Komatipoort, Veld-kornet Stefanus Malherbe was killed. So he never told us what the President had said in answer to his question about the Kruger millions.

The Red Coat

I have spoken before of some of the queer things that happen to your mind through fever (Oom Schalk Lourens said). In the past there was a good deal more fever in the Marico and Waterberg districts than there is today. And you got it in a much more severe form, too. Today you still get malaria in these parts, of course. But your temperature doesn't go so high any more before the fever breaks. And you are not left as weak after an attack of malaria as you were in the old days. Nor do you often get illusions of the sort that afterwards came to trouble the mind of Andries Visagie.

They say that this improvement is due to civilisation.

Well, I suppose that must be right. For one thing, we now have a government lorry from Zeerust every week with letters and newspapers and catalogues from Johannesburg shop-keepers. And only three years ago Jurie Bekker bought a wooden stand with a glass for measuring how much rain he gets on his farm. Jurie Bekker is very proud of his rain-gauge, too, and will accompany any white visitor to the back of his house to show him how well it works. 'We have had had no rain for the last three years,' Jurie Bekker will explain, 'and that is exactly what the rain-gauge records, also. Look, you can see for yourself – nil!'

Jurie Bekker also tried to explain the rain instrument to the kafirs on his farm. But he gave it up. 'A kafir with a blan-ket on hasn't got the brain to understand a white man's inventions,' Jurie Bekker said about it, afterwards. 'When I showed my kafirs what this rain-gauge was all about, they just stood in a long row and laughed.'

Nevertheless, I must admit that, with all this civilisation we are getting here, the malaria fever has not of recent years been the scourge it was in the old days.

The story of Andries Visagie and his fever begins at the battle of Bronkhorst Spruit. It was at the battle of Bronkhorst

Spruit that Andries Visagie had his life saved by Piet Niemand, according to all accounts. And yet it was also, arising out of that incident, that many people in this part of the Marico in later years came to the conclusion that Andries Visagie was somebody whose word you could not take seriously, because of the suffering that he had undergone.

You know of course, that the Bronkhorst Spruit battle was fought very long ago. In those days we still called the English 'redcoats'. For the English soldiers wore red jackets that we could see against the khaki colour of the tamboekie grass for almost as far as the bullets from our Martini-Henry rifles could carry. That shows you how uncivilised those times were.

I often heard Piet Niemand relate the story of how he found Andries Visagie lying unconscious in a donga on the battlefield, and of how he revived him with brandy that he had in his water-bottle.

Piet Niemand explained that, from the number of redcoats that were line up at Bronkhorst Spruit that morning, he could see it was going to be a serious engagement, and so he had thoughtfully emptied all the water out of his bottle and had replaced it with Magaliesberg peach brandy of the rawest kind he could get. Piet Niemand said that he was advancing against the English when he came across that donga. He was advancing very fast and was looking neither to right nor left of him, he said. And he would draw lines on any piece of paper that was handy to show you the direction he took.

I can still remember how annoyed we all were when a young schoolteacher, looking intently at that piece of paper, said that if that was the direction in which Piet Niemand was advancing, then it must have meant that the English had got right to behind the Boer lines, which was contrary to what he had read in the history books. Shortly afterwards Hannes Potgieter, who was chairman of our schoolcommittee, got that schoolteacher transferred.

As Hannes Potgieter said, that young schoolteacher with his history-book ideas had never been in a battle and didn't know what real fighting was. In the confusion of a fight, with guns going off all round you, Hannes Potgieter declared, it was not unusual for a burgher to find himself advancing away from the enemy – and quite fast, too.

He was not ashamed to admit that a very similar thing had happened to him at one stage of the battle of Majuba Hill. He had run back a long way, because he had suddenly felt that he wanted to make sure that the kafir *agterryers* were taking proper care of the horses. But he need have had no fears on that score, Hannes Potgieter added. Because when he reached the sheltered spot among the thorn-trees where the horses were tethered, he found that three commandants and a veldkornet had arrived there before him, on the same errand. The veldkornet was so anxious to reassure himself that the horses were all right, that he was even trying to mount one of them.

When Hannes Potgieter said that, he winked. And we all laughed. For we knew that he had fought bravely at Majuba Hill. But he was also ready always to acknowledge that he had been very frightened at Majuba Hill. And because he had been in several wars, he did not like to hear the courage of Piet Niemand called in question. What Hannes Potgieter meant us to understand was that if, at the battle of Bronkhorst Spruit, Piet Niemand did perhaps run at one stage, it was the sort of thing that could happen to any man; and for which any man could be forgiven, too.

And, in any case, Piet Niemand's story was interesting enough. He said that in the course of his advance he came across a donga, on the edge of which a thorn-bush was growing. The donga was about ten foot deep. He descended into the donga to light his pipe. He couldn't light his pipe out there on the open veld, because it was too windy, he said. When he reached the bottom of the donga, he also found that he had brought most of that thorn-bush along with him.

Then, in a bend of the donga, Piet Niemand saw what he thought was an English soldier, lying face downwards. He thought, at first, that the English soldier had come down there to light his pipe, also, and had decided to stay longer. He couldn't see too clearly, Piet Niemand said, because the smoke of the battle of Bronkhorst Spruit had got into his eyes. Maybe the smoke from his pipe, too, I thought. That is, if what he was lighting up there in the donga was Piet Retief roll tobacco.

Why Piet Niemand thought that the man lying at the bend of the donga was an Englishman was because he was wearing a red coat. But in the next moment Piet Niemand realised that the man was not an Englishman. For the man's neck was not also red.

Immediately there flashed into Piet Niemand's mind the suspicion that the man was a Boer in English uniform – a Transvaal Boer fighting against his own people. If it had been an Englishman lying there, he would have called on him to surrender, Piet Niemand said, but a Boer traitor he was going to shoot without giving him a chance to get up.

He was in the act of raising his Martini-Henry to fire, when the truth came to him. And that was how he first met Andries Visagie and how he came to save his life. He saw that while Andries Visagie's coat was indeed red, it was not with dye, but with the blood from his wound. Piet Niemand said that he was so overcome at the thought of the sin he had been about to commit that when he unstrapped his water-bottle his knees trembled as much as did his fingers. But when Piet Niemand told this part of his story, Hannes Potgieter said that he need not make any excuses for himself, especially as no harm had come of it. If it had been a Boer traitor instead of Piet Niemand who had found himself in that same situation, Hannes Potgieter said, then the Boer traitor would have fired in any case, without bothering very much as to whether it was a Boer or an Englishman that he was shooting.

Piet Niemand knelt down beside Andries Visagie and turned him round and succeeded in pouring a quantity of brandy down his throat. Andries Visagie was not seriously wounded, but he had a high fever, from the sun and through loss of blood, and he spoke strange words.

That was the story that Piet Niemand had to tell.

Afterwards Andries Visagie made a good recovery in the mill at Bronkhorst Spruit, that the commandant had turned into a hospital. And they say it was very touching to observe Andries Visagie's gratitude when Piet Niemand came to visit him.

Andries Visagie lay on the floor, on a rough mattress filled with grass and dried mealie-leaves. Piet Niemand went and sat on the floor beside him. They conversed. By that time Andries Visagie had recovered sufficiently to remember that he had shot three redcoats for sure. He added, however, that as the result of the weakness caused by his wound, his mind was not always very clear, at times. But when he got quite well and strong again, he would remember better. And then he would not be at all surprised if he remembered that he had also shot a general, he said.

Piet Niemand then related some of his own acts of bravery. And because they were both young men it gave them much pleasure to pass themselves off as heroes in each other's company.

Piet Niemand had already stood up to go when Andries Visagie reached his hand underneath the mattress and pulled out a watch with a heavy gold chain. The watch was shaped like an egg and on the case were pictures of angels, painted in enamel. Even without those angels, it would have been a very magnificent watch. But with those angels painted on the case, you would not care much if the watch did not go, even, and you still had to tell the time from the sun, holding your hand cupped over your eyes.

'I inherited this watch from my grandfather,' Andries Visagie said. 'He brought it with him on the Great Trek. You saved my life in the donga. You must take this watch as a keepsake.'

Those who were present at this incident in the temporary hospital at Bronkhorst Spruit said that Piet Niemand reached over to receive the gift. He almost had his hand on the watch, they say. And then he changed his mind and stood up straight.

'What I did was nothing,' Piet Niemand said. 'It was something anybody would have done. Anybody that was brave enough, I mean. But I want no reward for it. Maybe I'll some day buy myself a watch like that.'

Andries Visagie kept his father's father's egg-shaped watch, after all. But in his having offered Piet Niemand his most treasured possession, and in Piet Niemand having declined to accept it, there was set the seal on the friendship of those two young men. This friendship was guarded, maybe, by the wings of the angels painted in enamel on the watch-case. Afterwards people were to say that it was a pity Andries Visagie should have turned so queer in the head. It must have been that he had suffered too much, these people said.

In gratitude for their services in the first Boer War, the government of the Transvaal Republic made grants of farming land in the Waterberg district to those Boers on commando who had no ground of their own. The government of the Transvaal Republic did not think it necessary to explain that the area in question was already occupied – by lions and malaria mosquitoes and hostile kafirs. Nevertheless, many Boers knew the facts about that part of the Waterberg pretty well. So only a handful of burghers were prepared to accept government farms. Most of the others felt that, seeing they had just come out of one war, there was not much point in going straight back to another.

All the same, a number of burghers did go and take up land in that area, and to everybody's surprise – not least to the surprise of the government, I suppose – they fared reasonably well. And among those new settlers in the Waterberg were Piet Niemand and Andries Visagie. Their farms were not more than two days' journey apart. So you could almost say they were neighbours. They visited each other regularly.

The years went by, and then in a certain wet season Andries Visagie lay stricken with malaria. And in his delirium he said strange things. Fancying himself back again at Bronkhorst Spruit, Andries Visagie said he could remember the long line of English generals he was shooting. He was shooting them full of medals, he said.

But there was another thing that Andries Visagie said he remembered then. And after he recovered from the malaria he still insisted that the circumstance he had recalled during his illness was the truth. He said that through that second bout of fever he was able to remember what had happened years before, in the donga, when he was also delirious.

And it was then that many of the farmers in the Waterberg began to say what a pity it was that Andries Visagie's illness should so far have affected his mind.

For Andries Visagie said that he could remember distinctly, now, that time when he was lying in the donga. And he would never, of course, know who shot him. But what he did remember was that when Piet Niemand was bending over him, holding a water-bottle in his hand, Piet Niemand was wearing a redcoat.

Oom Tobie's Sickness

From the way he was muffled to the chin in a khaki overcoat and his wife's scarf in the heat of the day, we knew why Tobias Schutte was sitting on the riempies bench in Jurie Steyn's voorkamer. We knew that Tobias Schutte was going by lorry to Bekkersdal to get some more medical treatment. There was nobody in the Groot Marico who suffered as regularly and acutely from maladies – imaginary and otherwise – as did Tobias Schutte. For that reason he was known as 'Iepekonders Oom Tobie' from this side of the Pilanesberg right to the Kalahari: a good way into the Kalahari, sometimes – the exact distance depending on how far the Klipkop Bushmen had to go into the desert to find 'msumas.

You look to be in a pretty bad way again, Oom Tobie,' Chris Welman said in a tone that Oom Tobie accepted as implying sympathy. Nobody else in the voorkamer took it up that way, however. To the rest of us, Chris Welman's remark was just a plain sneer. 'What's it this time, Oom Tobie?' he went on, 'the miltsiek or St. Vitus's dance? But you got it while you were working, I'll bet.'

'Just before I started working, to be exact,' Oom Tobie replied. 'I was just getting ready to plant in the first pole for the new cattle camp when the sickness overtook me. Of a sudden I came all over queer. So I just had to leave the whole job to the Cape Coloured man, Pieterse, and the Bechuanas. The planting of the poles, the wiring, chasing away meerkats – I had to leave it all to them. They are at it now. I don't know what I'd do without Pieterse. I must give him an old pair of trousers again, one of these days. I've got a pair that are quite good still, except that they are worn out in the seat. It's queer how all my trousers get worn out like that, in the seat. The clothes you get today aren't what they used to be. I buy a new pair of trousers to wear when I go out on the lands, and before I know where I am they're frayed all thin, at the seat . . .'

'Was Pieterse – I mean, did Pieterse not look very surprised, sort of, at your being taken ill so suddenly, Oom Tobie?' Jurie Steyn asked, doing his best to keep a straight face.

'Well, no,' Oom Tobie replied in all honesty. 'When he helped me back on to the stoep from the place where we were going to put up the fence, Pieterse said he had felt for quite some days that I had this illness coming on. It wasn't so much anything he could see about me as what he *felt*, he said. And he could remember the exact time, too, when he first had that feeling. It was the afternoon when the poles and the rolls of barbed wire came from Ramoutsa. He didn't himself feel too good, either, that afternoon, he said. It was as though there was something unhealthy in the air. He's an extraordinary fellow, Pieterse. But that's because he's Cape Coloured, I suppose. I wouldn't be surprised if he's some part of him *Slams*, too. You know these Malays . . .'

Chris Welman asked Oom Tobie what he thought his illness was, this time.

'Well, I know it can't be the horse sickness,' Oom Tobie said, 'because I had the horse sickness last year. And when you've had the horse sickness once you don't get it again. You're salted.'

The new schoolteacher, Vermaak, who wasn't long out of college, and whom Jurie Steyn's wife seemed to think a lot of, on account of his education, then said that it was the first time he had ever heard of a human being getting horse sickness.

Several of us, speaking at the same time, told the schoolteacher that there were lots of things he had never heard of, and that a white man getting horse sickness was what he now had an opportunity of getting instructed about. We told him that if he remained in the Groot Marico longer, and observed a little, he would no doubt learn things that would surprise him, yet.

The schoolmaster said that that had already happened to him. Just from looking around, he said.

'What I have got this time, now, is, I think, the blue-tongue,' Oom Tobie continued. 'Mind you, I used to think that only sheep get the blue-tongue. When there is rain after a long drought – that is the worst time for blue-tongue. And you know the dry spell *was* pretty long, here in the district, before these rains started. So I think it must be blue-tongue.'

Gysbert van Tonder asked Oom Tobie to put his tongue out, so we could see. We all pretended to take a lot of interest in Oom Tobie's tongue, then. It was, of course, quite an ordinary-looking sort of tongue, perhaps somewhat on the thick side and with tobacco juice stains in the cracks. Oom Tobie first protruded his tongue out straight in front of his face as far as it would go – a by no means inconsiderable distance. Then he let his tongue hang down on his chin, for a bit.

Oom Tobie was engaged in lifting his tongue up again, in the direction of his eyebrows, so that we could see the underneath part of it, when Jurie Steyn's wife came into the voorkamer from the kitchen. From her remarks, then, it was clear that she had not heard any of our previous conversation.

'I am ashamed of you, Oom Tobie,' Jurie Steyn's wife announced, speaking very severely. 'Sticking out your tongue at Mr. Vermaak like that.'

The schoolmaster was sharing the riempies bench with Oom Tobie.

Oom Tobie started to explain what it was all about. But because he forgot, in the excitement of the moment, to put his tongue back, first, all he could utter was a sequence of somewhat peculiar noises.

'If you disagree with Mr. Vermaak on any subject,' Jurie Steyn's wife went on, 'then you can at least discuss the matter with him in a respectable sort of way. To stick out your tongue at a man, and to *wobble* it, is no way to carry on a discussion, Oom Tobie. I can only hope that Mr. Vermaak does not think *everybody* in the bushveld is so unrefined.'

By that time Oom Tobie had found his tongue again, however, in quite a literal way. And in a few simple sentences he was able to acquaint Jurie Steyn's wife with the facts of the situation. Oom Tobie might have made those sentences even simpler, perhaps. Only he happened, out of the corner of his eye, to catch a glimpse of Jurie Steyn behind the counter.

And Oom Tobie was sick enough on account of the blue-tongue. He did not want to become still more of an invalid as a result of a misunderstanding with Jurie Steyn's wife, who was known for his strength and ill-temper.

'But if it's the blue-tongue in sheep that I've got,' Oom Tobie proceeded, hastily, 'then it won't show first in my tongue, so much. You see it first in the limp sort of way my wool hangs. It was the same with the horse sickness. The first sign of it was a feeling of stiffness just behind the fetlock. It was several days before I started getting the snuffles . . .'

Gysbert van Tonder interrupted Oom Tobie at that point.

'Tell us, Oom Tobie . . .' Gysbert van Tonder began, and as he spoke his glance travelled in the direction of young Vermaak, the schoolteacher. We guessed what was going on in Gysbert van Tonder's mind. We felt the same way about it, too. You see, in the Marico we might perhaps laugh at Oom Tobie, and invent a nickname for him, and we didn't mind if the Klipkop tribe of Bushmen in the Kalahari spoke of him by that nickname. Those things we could understand. But even when we laughed at Oom Tobie, we also had a respect for him. And we didn't like the idea that a stranger straight from university, like young Vermaak, wearing city clothes and all, should not give Oom Tobie his due. For that matter, the Klipkop Bushmen still gave Oom Tobie his due. And *they* did not wear city clothes. Not by a long chalk the Klipkop Bushmen didn't.

And what we were genuinely proud of Oom Tobie about was the fact that he had had more wild and domestic animal diseases than any man you could come across anywhere in Africa. In that respect Oom Tobie was an important asset to the Marico. At catchweights and with no holds barred, we could put him, in his own line, against any sick man from Woodstock Beach to the Zambesi. And while we could laugh at him as much as we wanted, we did not like strangers to.

Consequently, when Gysbert van Tonder turned to Oom Tobie with a determined expression on his face, we knew what Gysbert was going to say. He was going to ask Oom Tobie, salted with horse sickness and all, *really* to show his paces.

'Tell us,' Gysbert van Tonder said, getting up from his chair and folding his arms across his chest. 'Tell us, Oom Tobie, about the time you had *snake* sickness.'

Thus encouraged, Oom Tobie told us, and with an elaborate amount of detail.

'But I wouldn't like to have to go through all that again,' he ended up. 'All the time I was suffering from snake disease I felt so *low*, if you understand what I mean. With my backside right on the ground, as it were.'

Chris Welman coughed, then.

For Jurie Steyn's wife was still present, and it seemed as though Oom Tobie was perhaps getting a bit coarse. To our surprise, however, Jurie Steyn himself said that it was quite in order. When you were talking about snakes, it was only natural that you should talk about them as they were, he said. It would be ungodly to pretend that a snake was different from what we all knew a snake to be.

He spoke with a warmth that made us feel uncomfortable.

'For that matter,' Jurie Steyn added, with a sort of careful deliberation, 'there is more than just one kind of snake right here in the Marico. There are *lots* of kinds.'

I noticed that the young schoolteacher looked down, when Jurie spoke like that. I also noticed that shortly afterwards Jurie Steyn's wife went back to the kitchen.

We were glad when Oom Tobie started talking about his illness again. It seemed to remove quite a lot of strain.

'Maybe it isn't the blue-tongue,' Oom Tobie said, 'because I felt it coming on even before the time that Pieterse spoke to me about it. I felt it after I had bought that barbed wire at the store at Ramoutsa. So I think maybe it's something I ate. I ate two bananas. They gave me those two bananas as a bonsella for all the wire I bought.'

Shortly afterwards the government lorry came. And I still remember what At Naude, who reads the newspapers, said when Oom Tobie, all buttoned up in his coat and scarf, and with a cushion under his arm, climbed aboard the lorry.

'Oom Tobie looks like he's a Member of Parliament,' At Naude said, 'fixed up for an all-night sitting.'

Nevertheless, we were not too happy when, next time the

lorry came, the driver told us what the doctor at Bekkersdal had told him was wrong with Oom Tobie. For it was a human disease, this time. And it would almost appear as though the Cape Coloured man, Pieterse, really was to some extent *Slams*. Moreover, we ourselves had been in somewhat close contact with Oom Tobie, and so we did not feel too comfortable about it.

It looked as though Oom Tobie had landed a winner, all right, and it was not impossible that the bonsella bananas had played a part in it.

All the same, it's queer how frightened everybody gets when you hear the word smallpox.

School Concert

The preparations for the annual school concert were in full swing.

In the Marico, these school concerts were held in the second part of June, when the nights were pleasantly cool. It was too hot, in December, for recitations and singing and reading the *Joernaal* that carried playful references to the activities and idiosyncrasies of individual members of the Dwarsberg population. On a midsummer's night, in a little school-building crowded to the doors with children and adults, and with more adults leaning in through the windows and keeping out the air, the songs and recitations sounded limp, somehow. Moreover, the personal references in the *Joernaal* did not sound quite as playful, then, as they were intended to be.

The institution of the *Joernaal* dated back to the time of the first Hollander schoolmaster in the Groot Marico. The *Joernaal* was a very popular feature of school concerts in Limburg, where he came from, the Hollander schoolmaster explained. For weeks beforehand the schoolmaster, assisted by some of the pupils in the upper class, would write down, in the funniest way they knew, odds and ends of things about people living in the neighbourhood. Why, they just about killed themselves laughing, while they were writing those things down in a class room in old Limburg, the Hollander schoolmaster said, and then, at the concert, one of the pupils would read it all out. Oh, it was a real scream. You wouldn't mention people's names, of course, the Hollander schoolmaster went on to say. You would just *hint* at who they were. It was all done in a subtle sort of way, naturally, but it was also clear enough so that you couldn't possibly miss the allusion. And you knew straight away who was *meant*.

That was what the first Hollander schoolmaster in the Marico explained, oh, long ago, before the reading, at a school concert, of the first Joernaal.

Today, in the Dwarsberge, they still talk about that concert.

It would appear, somehow, that in drawing up the *Joernaal,* the Hollander schoolmaster had not been quite subtle enough. Or, maybe, what they would split their sides laughing at in Limburg would raise quite different sorts of emotions north of the railway line to Ottoshoop. That's the way it is with humour, of course. Anyway, while the head pupil was reading out the *Joernaal* – stuttering a bit now and again because he could sense what that silence on the part of a bushveld audience meant – the Hollander schoolmaster had tears streaming down his cheeks, the way his laughter was convulsing him. Seated on the platform next to the pupil who was reading, the schoolmaster would reach into his pocket every so often for his handkerchief to wipe his eyes with. That made the audience freeze into a yet greater stillness.

A farmer's wife said afterwards that she felt she could just choke, then.

'If what was in that *Joernaal* were *jokes*, now,' Koos Kirstein – who had been a prominent cattle smuggler in his day – said, 'well I can laugh at a joke with the best of them. I read the page of jokes at the back of *Die Kerkbode* regularly every month. But can anybody see anything to titter at in asking where I got the money from to buy that harmonium that my daughter plays hymns on? That came in the *Joernaal.*'

Koos Kirstein asked that question of a church elder a few days after the school concert, and the elder said, no, there was nothing funny in it. Everybody in the Marico *knew* where Koos Kirstein got his money from, the elder said.

'And saying I am so well in with the police,' Koos Kirstein continued. 'Saying in the *Joernaal* that a policeman on border patrol went and hid behind my harmonium when a special plainclothes inspector from Pretoria walked into my voorkamer unexpectedly. Why, the schoolmaster just about doubled up laughing, when that bit was being read out.'

Anyway, the reading of that first *Joernaal* at a Marico school concert never reached to a proper end. When the proceedings terminated the head pupil still had a considerable number of unread foolscap sheets in his hand. And he was stuttering more than ever. For he had just finished the part about the Indian store at Ramoutsa refusing to give Giel Oosthuizen any more credit until he paid off something on last year's account.

Before that he had read out something about a crateful of muscovy ducks at the Zeerust market that Faans Lemmer had loaded on to his own wagon by mistake, and that he afterwards, still making the same error, unloaded into his own chicken pen – not noticing at the time, the difference between the muscovy ducks and his own Australorps – as he afterwards explained to the market master.

The head pupil had also read out something about why Frikkie Snyman's grandfather had to stay behind in the tent on the kerkplein when the rest of the family went to the Nagmaal. It wasn't the rheumatics that kept Frikkie Snyman's grandfather away from the Communion service, the *Joernaal* said, but he stayed behind in the tent because he didn't have an extra pair of laced-up shop boots. It was when Frikkie Snyman's wife, Hanna, knelt in church at the end of a pew and her long skirt that had all flowers on came up over one ankle – the *Joernaal* said – that you realised how Frikkie Snyman's grandfather was sitting barefooted in the tent on the kerkplein.

That was about as far as the head pupil got with the reading of the *Joernaal* . . . and to this day they can still show you, in an old Marico schoolroom, the burnt corner of a blackboard from where the lamp fell on it when the audience turned the platform upside down on the Hollander schoolmaster. Nothing happened to the head pupil, however. He sensed what was coming and got away, in time, into the rafters. Unlike most head-pupils, he had a quick mind.

All that happened very long ago, of course, as we were saying to each other in Jurie Steyn's post office. Today, the Marico was very different, we said to one another. Those old farmers didn't have the advantages that we enjoyed today, we said. There was no Afrikander Cattle Breeders' Society in those days, or even the Dwarsberge Hog Breeders' Society and you would never see a front garden with irises in it – or a front garden at all, for that matter. And you couldn't order clothes by post from Johannesburg, just filling in your measurements, so that all your wife had to do was . . .

But it was when Jurie Steyn's wife explained what she had to do to the last serge suit that Jurie Steyn ordered by post, just giving his size, that we saw that this example that we mentioned did not perhaps reflect progress in the Groot Marico in its best light.

From the way Jurie Steyn's wife spoke, it would seem that the easiest part of the alterations she had to make was cutting off the trouser turn-ups and inserting the material in the neck part of the jacket. 'And then the suit still hung on Jurie like a sack,' she concluded.

But Gysbert van Tonder said that she must not blame the Johannesburg store for it too much. There was something about the way Jurie Steyn was *built*, Gysbert van Tonder said. And we could not help noticing a certain nasty undertone in his voice, then, when he said that.

Johnny Coen smoothed the matter over very quickly, however. He had also had difficulties, ordering suits by post, he said. But he found it helped the Johannesburg store a lot if you sent a full-length photograph of yourself along with the order. They always returned the photograph. No, Johnny Coen said in reply to a question from At Naude, he didn't know *why* that Johannesburg store sent the photographs back so promptly, under registered cover and all. And then, when he saw that At Naude was laughing, Johnny Coen said that that firm could, perhaps, if it wanted to, keep all those photographs and frame them. But, all the same, he added, it would help the shop a lot if, next time Jurie Steyn ordered a suit by post, he also put in a full-length photograph of himself.

But all this talk was getting us away from what we had been saying about how more broad-minded the Groot Marico had become since the old days, due to progress. It was then that

Koos Nienaber brought us back to what we were discussing.

'Where our forefathers in the Marico were different from the way we are today,' Koos Nienaber said, 'is because they hadn't learnt to laugh at themselves, yet. They took themselves much too seriously. Although they had to, I suppose, since it was all going to be put into history books. But we today are different. We wouldn't carry on in an undignified manner if, at the next concert, there should be something in the *Joernaal* to show up our little weaknesses. We would laugh, I mean. Take Jurie Steyn and his serge suit, now. Well, we've got a sense of humour, today. I mean, Jurie Steyn would be the first to laugh at how funny he looks in that serge suit –'

'How do you mean I look funny in my new suit?' Jurie Steyn demanded.

At Naude came in between the two of them, then, and made it clear to Jurie Steyn that Koos Nienaber had been saying those things merely by way of argument, and to prove his point. Koos Nienaber didn't mean that Jurie Steyn actually *looked* funny in his new suit, At Naude explained.

'If he doesn't mean it, what does he want to say it for?' Jurie Steyn said, sounding only half convinced. 'And anyway, Koos Nienaber needn't talk. When he came round with the collection plate at the last Nagmaal, and he was wearing his new manel, I thought Koos Nienaber was an orang-utan.'

Nevertheless, we all acknowledged at the end that we were looking forward to the school concert. And there should be quite a lot of fun in having the *Joernaal,* we said. Seeing how today we had a sense of humour.

School Concert II

It was not only schoolchildren and their parents that came to attend the concert in that little school building of which the middle partition had been taken away to make it into one hall. For instance, there was Hendrik Prinsloo, who had come all the way from Vleispoort by Cape cart, and had not meant to attend the concert at all, since he was on his way to Zeerust and was just passing that way, when some of the parents persuaded him, for the sake of his horses, to outspan under the thorn trees on the school grounds by the side of the government road.

It was observed that Hendrik Prinsloo had a red face and that he mistook one of the swingle-bars for the step when he alighted from the Cape cart. So – after they had looked to see what was under the seat of the Cape cart – several of the farmers present counselled Hendrik Prinsloo to rest awhile by the roadside, seeing it was already getting on towards evening. They also sent a Native over to At Naude's house for glasses, instructing him to be as quick as he liked. And if At Naude didn't have glasses, cups would do, one of the farmers added, thoughtfully. By the look of things it was going to be a good children's concert, they said.

Meanwhile the schoolroom was filling up quite nicely. There had been some talk, during the past few days, that a scientist from the Agricultural Research Insitute, who was known to be in the neighbourhood, would distribute the school prizes at the concert and also give a little lecture on his favourite subject, which was correct winter-grazing. Even that rumour did not keep people away, however. They had the good sense to guess that it was only a rumour, anyhow. Afterwards it was found out that it had been started by Chris Welman, because the schoolmaster had turned down Chris Welman's offer to sing 'Boereseun', with actions, at the concert.

There was loud applause when young Vermaak, the schoolmaster, came on to the platform. His black hair was neatly parted in the middle and his city suit of blue serge looked very smart in the lamp light. You could hardly notice those darker patches on the jacket to which Jurie Steyn's wife drew attention, when she said that you could see where Alida van Niekerk had again been trying to clean the schoolmaster's suit with paraffin. Vermaak was boarding at the Van Niekerk's, and Alida was their eldest daughter.

The schoolmaster said he was glad to see that there was such a considerable crowd tonight, including quite a number of fathers, whom he knew personally, who were looking in at the windows. There were still a few vacant seats for them inside, he said, if they would care to come in. But Gysbert van Tonder, speaking on behalf of those fathers said, no, they did not mind being self-sacrificing in that way. It was not right that the schoolroom should be cluttered up with a lot of fat, healthy men, over whose heads the smaller children would not be able to see properly. There was also a neighbour of theirs, from Vleispoort, Hendrik Prinsloo, who was resting a little. And they wanted to keep an eye on his Cape cart, which was standing there all by itself in the dark. If the schoolmaster looked out of that nearest window he would be able to *see* that lonely Cape cart, Gysbert van Tonder said.

Young Vermaak, who didn't know what was going on, seemed touched at this display of solicitude for a neighbour by just simple-hearted bushveld farmers. Several of the wives of those farmers sniffed, however.

Three little boys carrying little riding whips and wearing little red jackets came on to the platform and the schoolmaster explained that they would sing a hunting song called 'Jan Pohl', which had been translated from English by the great Afrikaans poet, Van Blerk Willemse. Everybody agreed that the translation was a far superior cultural work to the original, the schoolmaster said. In fact you wouldn't recognise that it was the same song, even, if it wasn't for the tune. But that would also be put right shortly, the schoolmaster added. The celebrated Afrikaans composer, Frik Dinkelman, was going to get to work on it.

At Naude said to the other fathers standing at the window that that man in the song, Jan Pohl, must be a bit queer in the head. 'Wearing a red jacket and with a riding whip and a bugle to go and shoot a ribbok in the rante,' At Naude said.

Another father pointed out that that Jan Pohl didn't even have such a thing as a Native walking along in front, through the tamboekie grass, where there was always a likelihood of mambas.

The next item on the programme was a group of boys and girls, in pairs pirouetting about the platform to the music of 'Pollie, Ons Gaan Pêrel Toe.' Since many of the parents were Doppers, the schoolmaster took the trouble first to explain that what the children were doing wasn't really *dancing* at all. They were stepping about, quickly, sort of, in couples, kind of, to the measure of a polka in a manner of speaking. It was Volkspele, and had the approval of the Synod, the schoolmaster said. All the same, a few of the more earnest members of the audience kept their eyes down on the floor, while that was going on. They also refrained, in a quite stern manner, from beating time to the music with their feet.

For that reason it came as something of a relief when, at the end of the Volkspele, a number of children with wide blue collars trooped on to the stage. They were going to sing 'Die Vaal se Bootman'. It was really a Russian song, the schoolmaster explained. But the way the great Afrikaans poet Van Blerk Willemse had handled it, you wouldn't think it at all. Maybe why it was such an outstanding translation, the schoolmaster said, was because Van Blerk Willemse didn't know any Russian, and didn't want to either.

The song was a great success. The audience were still humming 'Yo-ho-yo' to themselves a good way into the next item on the programme.

Meanwhile, the fathers outside the school building had deserted their places by the windows and had drifted in the direction of the Cape cart to make sure that everything was still in order there. And they sat down on the ground as close as they could get to the Cape cart, to make sure that things stayed in order. One of the fathers, still singing 'Yo-ho-yo' even went and sat right on top of Hendrik Prinsloo's face, without noticing anything wrong. Hendrik Prinsloo didn't notice anything, either, at first, but when he did he made such a fuss, shouting 'Elephants' and such-like, that At Naude, who had remained at the schoolroom window, came running up to the Cape cart, fearing the worst.

'Is that all?' At Naude asked, when it was explained to him what had happened. 'From the way Hendrik Prinsloo was carrying on, I thought some clumsy —' he used a strong word, 'some clumsy — had kicked over the jar.'

In the meantime Hendrik Prinsloo had risen to a half-sitting posture, with his hand up to his face. 'Feel here, kêrels,' he said. 'The middle part of my face has suddenly gone all flat, and my jaw is all sideways. Just feel here.'

The farmers around the Cape cart were fortunately able – in between singing 'Yo-ho-yo' – to set Hendrik Prinsloo's mind at rest. He was worrying about nothing at all, they assured him. His face had always been that way.

Nevertheless, Hendrik Prinsloo did not appear to be as grateful as he should have been for that explanation. He said quite a lot of things that we felt did not fit in with a school concert.

'The schoolmaster says the *Joernaal* is going to be read out shortly,' At Naude announced. 'Well, I hope there is going to be nothing in it like the sort of things Hendrik Prinsloo is saying now. All the same, I wonder what there is going to be in the *Joernaal* – you know what I mean – funny stories about people we all know.'

Gysbert van Tonder started telling us about a *Joernaal* that he had once heard read out at a Nagelspruit school concert. A deputation of farmers saw the schoolmaster on to the government lorry immediately afterwards, Gysbert van Tonder said. The schoolmaster's clothes and books they sent after him, carriage forward, next day.

'I wonder, though,' At Naude said, 'will young Vermaak mention in the *Joernaal* about himself and – and – you know who I mean – that *will* be a laugh.'

As it turned out, however, there was no mention of that in the *Joernaal.* Nor was there any reference, direct or indirect, to anybody else in the Marico, either. In compiling the *Joernaal,* all that the schoolmaster had done was to cut a whole lot of jokes out of back numbers of magazines and to include also some funny stories that had been popular in the Marico for many years, and for generations, even. And because there is nothing that you enjoy as much as hearing an old joke for the hundredth time, the *Joernaal* got the audience into a state of uproarious good humour.

It was all so *jolly* that Jurie Steyn's wife did not even say anything sarcastic when Alida van Niekerk went and picked up the schoolmaster's programme, that had dropped on to the floor, for him.

The concert in the schoolroom went on until quite late, and everybody said how successful it was. The concert at the Cape cart, which nearly all the fathers joined in, afterwards, was perhaps even more successful, and lasted a good deal longer. And Chris Welman did get his chance, there, to sing 'Boereseun' with actions.

And when Hendrik Prinsloo drove off eventually, in his Cape cart, into the night, there was hand-shaking all round, and they cheered him, and everybody asked him to be sure and come round again to the next school concert, also.

Next day there was only the locked door of the old school building to show that it was the end of term.

And at the side of a footpath that a solitary child walked along to and from school lay fragments of a torn-up quarterly report.

... at this time of year

It was always about now, Jurie Steyn said, with the year drawing to an end, that he got all sorts of queer feelings. He didn't know how to say them, quite. But one feeling he did get, and that he had no difficulty in explaining, he said, was a homesickness to be back again in the Western Province where he had spent his early childhood.

Jurie Steyn heaved a medium-length sigh, then, thinking back on the years when he was young.

'Not that I haven't got a deep love for the Transvaal,' Jurie Steyn added, in case we should get him wrong, 'I am after all, a Transvaler –'

And so we said, yes, it was quite all right. We understood his feelings for the old Cape Colony. He needn't explain, we said.

'And because I've said that I passed my young years in the Cape,' Jurie Steyn went on, the suggestion of a combative look coming into his eyes, 'that doesn't mean to say that I am old, today.'

We hastened to reassure him on that point, too – but not very convincingly, it seemed. Gysbert van Tonder even coughed.

'I know what you mean, Jurie,' young Johnny Coen said, quickly, hastening to forestall any unpleasantness that might ensue on Jurie Steyn demanding of Gysbert van Tonder what he meant by clearing his throat, that way. 'It's the place where you were born and bred and you can't ever forget. I was born in the Marico bushveld, and you've got no idea how homesick I got the time I was working on the railway at Ottoshoop.

'But of course, Ottoshoop is at least ninety miles from here – even, if you don't go the road through Sephton's Nek. So I know how you feel, Jurie. No matter how kind people are to you even, if they're not your own people you do get very lonely, sometimes. Oh, yes, I went through all that at Ottoshoop.'

Johnny Coen went on to describe a wedding reception that he had attended at Ottoshoop while he was an exile in those parts.

'They had spread white table-cloths over long tables on the front stoep,' Johnny Coen said. 'And there was a man at the party who did balancing tricks with a chair and a wine-glass. And I got more and more sad. The only time I laughed a little was when the loose seat dropped out of the chair and caught the man on the back of his neck when he was at the same time throwing up two guavas and a fork.'

Johnny Coen went on to say that, as it turned out, his neighbour at table was also a foreigner.

'How I knew,' Johnny Coen said, 'was when that man spoke to me. And he said I was looking pretty miserable. And he asked was it that I was in love with the bride, perhaps, and that another man had taken her away from me. And I said, no, I was from the Dwarsberge part of Marico, and I felt most homesick for Groot Marico when the people around me were most happy, I said. And that was how I got talking to that Englishman sitting next to me at the table. And when somebody in the voorkamer started playing "Home, Sweet Home" on the harmonium we were both of us crying on to the table-cloth. And I never used to think that an Englishman had any feelings, until then.

'Another thing I found out afterwards that I had in common with the Englishman was that he didn't like that man with the balancing tricks, either.'

Thereupon Jurie Steyn said that he, too, wouldn't like it very much if somebody were to start playing 'Home, Sweet Home' on a harmonium at this time of the year. Of course, he knew it best as a German song, Jurie Steyn said, and it was called 'Heimat Susse Heimat'. But the tune was the same. He had heard the German missionaries at Kronendal sing it quite often. And they would cry on to the thick slices of that kind of red sausage that they had on their plates, Jurie said.

'Take the Cape at this time of year, now,' Jurie Steyn said, 'in the summer.'

So we said, very well, we would take the Cape, then, if he put it like that.

'Well, when it gets towards about now, towards about Christmas time and the end of the year,' Jurie Steyn proceeded, 'why, I just can't help it. I think of a little Boland dorp with white houses and water furrows at the side of the streets and oak trees. Not that I haven't got all the time in the world for a moepel or a maroela or a kremetart or any other kind of bushveld tree. For instance, I have often walked to the end of my farm by the poort, just to go and look at the withaaks there. No, it isn't that. After all, an oak isn't a proper South African tree, even, but just imported.

'All the same, when it gets towards Christmas, the thought of those oak trees in the Cape comes into my mind just all of a sudden, sort of. And I get the feeling of how much nobler a kind of person I was in those days than what I am today. I think of how much more upright I was in my youth.'

Thereupon Gysbert van Tonder said, yes, *that* he could well believe.

We knew that Gysbert van Tonder – who was Jurie Steyn's neighbour – was hinting about the last bit of neighbourly unpleasantness they had, which had to do with the impounding of a number of stray oxen. And we didn't want to have *that* long argument all over again. Especially not with the Christmas season drawing near, and all.

It was quite a good thing, therefore, that Oupa Bekker should have started talking then about a quite ordinary camelthorn tree that grew on one end of Bekkersdal when it was first laid out as a dorp.

'It was because of what Jurie Steyn said about oaks that made me think of it,' Oupa Bekker said. 'I was there when Bekkersdal was proclaimed as a township, and the bush was cleared away and the surveyor measured out the streets and divided up the erfs. And the Commandant-General and the Dominee had words about whether the plein in the middle of the dorp should be for the Dopper Church, with a pastorie next to it, or for the Dopper Church, with a house for the Commandant-General's son-in-law next to it, a site to be chosen for the pastorie that would be within easy walking distance for the Dominee.'

Oupa Bekker said that in the end the Dominee decided that he wouldn't mind walking a little distance. Oupa Bekker said he had no doubt that what made the Dominee come to that decision was because the Dominee did not wish to make the Commandant-General unhappy.

For it was well known throughout the Northern Transvaal that few things made the Commandant-General so unhappy as when he had to take firm steps against anybody who opposed him. And Oupa Bekker said it was also known that on occasion the Commandant-General had taken steps that you might call even unusually firm against a person who stood in his way.

'And so the Dominee, agreed, in the end,' Oupa Bekker continued, 'that a short brisk walk from his pastorie to the church, of a Sunday morning before the sermon, would be healthful for him. And so a house for the Commandant-General was built on the measured-out erf on the plein next to the church. But all that happened – oh, so many years ago.'

Oupa Bekker's sigh would have been more prolonged than Jurie Steyn's had been. Only, because of his advanced years, Oupa Bekker didn't have the breath for it.

'All the same, that was a funny thing,' Chris Welman commented, 'for the old days, that is. And so I suppose that's the reason why –'

Oupa Bekker nodded.

For we knew where the pastorie was, today, in Bekkersdal. And we knew that the present-day minister, Dominee Welthagen, had to walk a fairish distance to church, of a Sunday, just as his predecessor of three-quarters of a century ago had to do. But that first Dominee would no doubt have been able to take short cuts, since at that time Bekkersdal would not have been as built up as it was today.

'And that erf that was measured out for the Commandant-General's son-in-law –' Chris Welman started to remark.

'Yes, that's the reason for all that trouble there, now,' Oupa Bekker said. 'But the old people always knew that the Commandant-General's son-in-law was a bit thoughtless. All those empty bottles that used to lie in his back yard, for instance. And that back yard isn't any more tidy today. Not with all those empty jam tins and all that garbage and all those empty fruit boxes lying in it. Why that back yard looks worse than ever, now that it has been taken over for an Indian store. And right next to the Dopper Church, and all. No wonder there's that trouble about it in Bekkersdal, now.'

So, we said, it was very sinful of the first Indian – who was the grandfather of the present Indian – to have gone and bought that erf right next to the Dopper Church to go and open an Indian store on.

There should really have been a pastorie there, we said.

'Bit of a pity the Commandant-General's son-in-law drank so much,' Johnny Coen observed.

In the discussion that followed about what a scandal it was that there should be an Indian store next to the Dopper Church in Bekkersdal, Oupa Bekker was able only in an edgeways fashion to tell us about the camel-thorn tree that grew at the edge of the Bekkersdal township. And we were not able to pay much attention to Oupa Bekker's story, then. Whereas it was quite a pretty story.

It appears that the streets of the newly-laid dorp were planted with jacarandas – an imported tree then coming into fashion. And at the end of one street, in exact line with the jacarandas, and at the same distance from its nearest jacaranda neighbour as the jacarandas were set apart from each other, there grew that indigenous old African camel-thorn tree.

And although the street ended just before it came to him, the old camel-thorn tree really imagined that he was part of that jacaranda avenue. And he was as pleased as anything about it. And he started putting on side, there, just as though he was also an imported tree, and not just an old camel-thorn that the veld was full of. And even though the municipality didn't water him, like they watered the jacaranda, the camel-thorn remained as cheerful as ever. He knew he didn't *need* watering.

Anyway, the point of Oupa Bekker's story had to do with the first summer that the jacarandas in Bekkersdal came to flowering. And one night there was a terrible wind from the Kalahari, so that in the morning the sidewalks were thickly strewn with purple flowers, and there were more jacaranda blooms stuck on the thorns of the old camel-thorn tree than any jacaranda still had on its branches, then. And the purple blossoms lay thick about the lower part of the gnarled trunk of the camel-thorn. It was his hour, and so you couldn't tell him from an imported tree.

We didn't hear very much of what Oupa Bekker had to say, however. We were too busy thinking out the right words for a strong letter we were drafting to our Member in Parliament. It had to do with the Indian Problem.

But it was after the railway lorry from Bekkersdal had drawn up at the front door that Gysbert van Tonder really let himself go on the Indian Problem. It was when Gysbert found out that the roll of barbed wire he had ordered wasn't on the lorry.

'It's the fault of the Indian storekeeper's assistant,' the lorry driver explained although he used a different word in referring to the young Indian who was helping the old Indian in the Bekkersdal store.

'I could see that the young Indian assistant wasn't himself. The shop was all done out with Christmas stockings, and things. And that old gramophone they've got at the back of the shop was playing "Home, Sweet Home". And that young Indian assistant was busy crying on to the counter. 'Saying that at this time of the year he always got homesick for Natal, the Indian assistant said. Well, beats me, all right. How anybody can ever feel homesick for Natal, I just don't know.'

Politics and Love

On the blackboard that you could see every time the speaker moved his head to one side was a mulplication sum: 973 x 8 = . There had been a number there, after the equals, but the schoolmaster had rubbed it out quickly, before the first members of the audience filed into the class room for the meeting.

It was just possible that the answer wasn't quite correct, the schoolmaster reflected, and he didn't want any nonsense about it from some busybody, afterwards.

The schoolmaster did not feel called upon to erase, from the blackboard, a brief statement to do with the geographical regions traversed by the Vaal River.

Thus it came about that every time Lennep van Ploert, the representative for Bekkersdal, moved his head to one side or the other, or bent forward to think – which he did not appear to do very deeply – there was revealed behind him, on the blackboard, in addition to the arithmetic, this sentence whose truth few would question, or, rather (this being a political meeting) would cavil at: 'The Vaal River is in Africa.'

Lennep van Ploert wore a black suit and a high, stick-up collar. And his voice was just as impressive as his looks. Many of the farmers and their wives present at the meeting had received their education in that same class room and sitting on those same benches. Consequently, more than one member of the audience identified Lennep van Ploert in his mind with the Hollander school-inspector who had come round annually to tell the pupils whether they had passed or failed.

There was a good attendance of farmers and their wives and children from the Rooibokspruit area to hear Lennep van Ploert report, in that schoolroom that served for a night as a political party venue, on the way he had furthered his constituents' interests during the past year in a building of more imposing dimensions than the schoolhouse, and with statelier portals.

Another point of difference between the two buildings was that in the Marico schoolroom the older pupils seldom threw chalk, any more. Most of them had also learnt to reject the cruder formularies of comedy built up around the placing of drawing pins on the schoolmaster's chair.

'And so in your interests I went and had tea with the Marquis de Monfiche,' the voice of Lennep van Ploert boomed. 'And while I was drinking tea with that distinguished French aristocrat and insurance representative –'

'Are you sure it was tea?' a man in a khaki shirt sitting at the back of the class room interjected.

A couple of people in the audience giggled. Others said 'Sh—.' Among the latter was the wife of a wealthy local cattle-smuggler. She was hoping that Lennep van Ploert would go on to say how the wife of the distinguished French marquis was dressed.'

The only person who was in no way embarrassed was the speaker himself. The remark made by the man in the khaki shirt was of a pattern accepted as wit in that other building (the one with the proud traditions and the coat-of-arms over the front stoep). Lennep van Ploert felt at home, then.

'No, it wasn't tea,' the speaker said, 'it was a milkshake.'

In that noble edifice in which Lennep van Ploert shone as a debater, such a brilliant piece of repartee would have received due appreciation. Grim features would have relaxed in smiles. A policeman wearing white gloves would have gone to the assistance of an elderly legislator who was in stitches through laughing.

There would have been jovial shouts of 'Withdraw!' There would have been a row of stipples in Hansard, the shorthand reporter not being able to get down the next couple of sentences on account of his emotions being so mixed. And afterwards, in the lobby, even some of Lennep van Ploert's opponents would have come and grasped Lennep van Ploert by the hand.

But, singularly enough, in that Marico schoolroom with the white-washed walls and the thatched roof and with no inspiring statuary on the premises – unless a child's clay model on a window-sill, of Adam with a pipe and braces, could fit into that category (one of Adam's braces having slipped off his shoulder on to a level with his knee) – in that Marico class room there was no immediate response of the sort that Lennep van Ploert had looked for.

Instead, the audience started wondering if there was something that they had missed, perhaps, in what Lennep van Ploert had just said. Or was he taking them to be just a lot of simpletons, because they were living out in the most northern part of the bushveld that you could live in and still be allowed to vote?

The only positive reaction, however, came from the man in the khaki shirt. He vacated his place at the back of the school room and moved up to a seat nearer the front.

'After I had signed the insurance papers for an endowment policy,' Lennep van Ploert proceeded, 'the French marquis said he would be honoured if my wife and I would visit him at his chateau next time we were in France. He did not know exactly when he would be going back to France, though. The marquis told me straight out that there was something about South Africa he *liked*. Anyway, I told him that, speaking on behalf of my constituents, I would accept his invitation.' (Applause.)

The man in the khaki shirt had been sitting between a young fellow with a blue and orange tie and a young girl with a selons rose in her hair.

The young man looked sideways at the girl and even in the uncertain light of the paraffin lamps the flush on his face was evident. The redness extended to the top part of his ears.

'I can't hear too well from there,' moving into the seat vacated by the man with the khaki shirt.

The girl did not answer.

'Is he – is he your father?' the young man enquired in a faltering voice, at the same time indicating the man in the khaki shirt, who was then engaged in feeling through his trousers pockets, thereby occasioning noticeable discomfort to the farmer sitting next to him, by reason of the confinement imposed by the school bench.

'He's my uncle,' the girl answered. 'I stay with him. I lost my parents when I was young.'

'I have before today tried to speak to you,' the young fellow with the blue and orange tie went on. 'But he was always with you.'

'I know,' the girl answered, unconsciously putting her hand up to the selons rose in her hair.

'At Zeerust with the last Nagmaal, now,' the young man went on. 'By the side of the kerkplein.'

'Yes,' the girl responsed simply.

'Only, your uncle kicked out, then, at —' the young man proceeded.

'He kicked just at a wild berry,' the girl explained. 'He's been like that since he came back from the mines.'

'Well, I just didn't understand, then,' the young man said. 'My name is Dawie Louw. What's yours?'

'Lettie,' the girl answered.

'Well, it was because your uncle kicked out, like that,' Dawie Louw went on, 'that I didn't –'

'Didn't come up and speak to us,' Lettie helped him out.

'Yes, and I think Lettie is a lovely name,' the young fellow said.

'And I like the name Dawie, also,' the girl said in a soft voice.

'And there was another time when I nearly came up and spoke to you,' Dawie Louw went on. 'It was right in front of –'

'Solly's hardware store,' Lettie said. 'Next to the four-disc harrows.'

From her voice it sounded like it was the rose garden of the Capulets under a Veronese moon.

'That's right,' Dawie Louw said. 'Only your uncle was again with you, and just when I was coming up, after pulling my tie straight – it was a purple tie with –'

'Green spots,' Lettie announced, looking slightly pained.

'Well,' Dawie Louw said, 'just as I was coming up, your uncle –'

'Kicked out at a four-disc harrow's disc,' Lettie said. 'That's another habit my uncle has brought back from the mines. He also carries a bicycle chain, through having lived in Fordsburg.'

Meanwhile, on the platform, Lennep van Ploert was continuing with his report to his constituents of his legislative activities.

'—wlawlawski,' Lennep van Ploert was saying. 'And it was coffee I had with him, that time, I mean with that distinguished Polish prince, who happened to have a few shares in a washing-machine company to dispose of, at the moment, and that I purchased. He invited me, on behalf of my constituents, to drop in at his palace in Poland whenever I was passing that way. But he didn't think he would go back there himself quite soon, the prince said. For one thing, he *liked* South Africa, he said. And he also mentioned something about their just *waiting* for him to come back, in his native country of Poland.'

The man in the khaki shirt, Lettie's uncle, spoke up for himself, then.

'Could they give my trousers a bit of a press?' he asked. 'That Polish washing-machine company of yours, that is?'

At the same time the man in the khaki shirt got up and moved to a seat that was still nearer the front.

'Has your uncle had –' Dawie Louw asked of Lettie.

'A few too many? Yes, I think so. It's since,' Lettie said, once more, 'he's come back from the mines.'

Dawie Louw asked the girl with the selons rose in her hair if she didn't think it was a queer thing that, after all that, they should at last have the chance of meeting and of talking to each other, sitting right next to each other in a school-bench, even.

He was young and sanguine, then, and he didn't know that a school-bench actually was the right place where two young lovers should meet. For who would yet have more to learn of the ways of the world than a boy and a girl in love?

'Praat politiek,' somebody shouted out to Lennep van Ploert. It was not the man in the khaki shirt (Lettie's uncle) that shouted. It was some other farmer, who had come to hear about policy and about election promises, and who couldn't understand that Lennep van Ploert, who had been such a firebrand a few years before, should now be content to hand out milksop stuff. For Lennep van Ploert was now talking about when he had cocoa with a Spanish nobleman who did a spot of real estate agency work in his spare time.

Lennep van Ploert leant forward to think, for a few moments, then.

And so Dawie Louw and Lettie were able to see what was written on the blackboard. And they spelt out, between them, the statement that the Vaal River was in Africa. And they laughed – just for no reason at all. They did not know that they would have been far better occupied in working out that arithmetic sum, instead. But young people in love don't know better.

'The first time I saw you was at the fat-stock sale at Schooneesdrif,' Dawie Louw said to Lettie. 'You were with your uncle and you wouldn't look at me.'

'The first time I saw you' Lettie said, 'was before Schooneesdrif.'

'At Schooneesdrif you had a frock with –' Dawie Louw started again.

But it was as much at Lettie's suggestion as his own that they slipped out of the door of the classroom, then, the two of them together, hand in hand. And they stood like that, a long time hand in hand, in silence, under the unclothed stars.

That was how they came to miss the unhappy incidents that took place inside the schoolroom a little later. For the man in the khaki shirt (Lettie's uncle) had eventually found what he was looking for, in his trousers pocket. But he was pulled off Lennep van Ploert before he could assault him to any serious purpose with his bicycle chain. But before that Lettie's uncle had borne the legislator back against the blackboard.

And that was how the meeting ended. And, strangely enough although Lennep van Ploert represented, for many members of the audience, the school-inspector of their youth, they were not unwilling to forgive the man in the khaki shirt for having dealt with him in that fashion.

Because of the way he had been pressed backwards against the blackboard by Lettie's uncle you were able to read afterwards on Lennep van Ploert's suit – the figures being the wrong way around – part of a sum in arithmetic. What was also legible on Lennep van Ploert's jacket – reading from right to left – was a chalked statement to the effect that the Vaal River flows in Africa.

But of neither of these circumstances did Dawie Louw and Lettie know anything. They stood at the side of the school house, holding hands under the stars. And they were young. And they were in love. And they were foolish. And they would not have cared about what vital sort of decision any statesman would have arrived at, then.

And they would have laughed about any Parallel that any general might have decided to cross.

Forbidden Country

'But surely the shortest way,' At Naude said, with reference to yet another expedition from overseas that was setting out for the Kalahari, 'would be for them to go through Ramoutsa and then through the Tsifulu –'

'Not so fast,' Chris Welman interrupted him. 'The expedition from abroad can't go through that part of the Tsifulu just as fast as you're saying it now, At.'

'Not through the Tsifulu,' Chris Welman concurred.

'The Tsifulu is forbidden country,' Gysbert van Tonder explained.

'Forbidden country,' Chris Welman echoed.

'It's forbidden to go through there,' Gysbert van Tonder repeated. In case he wasn't properly understood the first time.

'Forbidden,' came from Chris Welman with the sombre inevitability of a one-man Greek chorus.

Oh, that, At Naude said. That sort of thing just made him tired. We all knew the Tsifulu was called the Forbidden Country, At Naude said. But it was just a name given to that part. It didn't mean anything. It was just like Gysbert van Tonder's farm being called Paradise Kloof.

He could picture the surprise of a visitor to Gysbert van Tonder's farm, At Naude continued, that visitor going by just the name of the farm, and then that visitor suddenly seeing who it was sitting on the front stoep drinking coffee. Seeing Gysbert van Tonder sitting there, the visitor would think that he had come to the exact opposite place of paradise, At Naude said.

But Jurie Steyn said that he was in agreement with Gysbert van Tonder and Chris Welman. As long as he had been in the Marico he had known that that section of the Tsifulu was the Forbidden Country. And that was enough for him, Jurie Steyn said. If it was, as At Naude claimed, just a name, then why did it have that name?

'If the place is all right,' Jurie Steyn added, 'why don't they call it by a name like "Potluck Corner", or something meaning "Home From Home", say? Maybe that part of the Tsifulu isn't really forbidden, but I've never been around to look. The name is enough for me. I can take a hint as well as the next man, I suppose.'

Young Vermaak, the schoolmaster, said, then that he had also heard that there was that part, there, known as the Forbidden Country. He had never given it much thought, he said, but now that mention was being made of it, well, it did seem interesting to him as to how it should have got its name in the first place. Since Oupa Bekker was the oldest inhabitant of the Groot Marico, did Oupa Bekker know, perhaps?

But Oupa Bekker said, no, during all his years in those parts he had just always known of that section of the Tsifulu as being the Forbidden Country. How it got the name, he would not presume to guess, Oupa Bekker said.

'One thing, though,' he added. 'In the old days, when you spoke of the Forbidden Country, you would say it with more of a respect for it in your voice, sort of. You would also, as likely as not, take your hat off, then, without thinking, even.'

That made it sound yet more interesting, young Vermaak said. 'But that expedition from overseas, now,' he asked. 'How will they be able to tell, when they come to the Tsifulu, what part of it is forbidden? Why can't they go just straight through it? I don't suppose they've got notice boards up there to say "Forbidden Country – No Visitors" or "This Area Taboo – Keep out". Not that it would help much, I should think, putting up notice boards like that.

'Because, seeing what human nature is, even if the expedition had no intention of going through there, just to be told they weren't allowed in would awaken their curiosity. You can't beat just a plain word like "Unholy" for getting you really interested. I mean, it sounds much more inviting than "Pull In Here For a Nice Cup of Tea".'

The schoolmaster was partly right, Gysbert van Tonder said. It was indeed a truth that there were no notice-boards up. Furthermore, it was all mostly nothing more than thorn-trees and sand in that part, so that, just to lòok at, you would hardly even know which was the Forbidden Country area and which wasn't.

'But all the same you don't need notice-boards,' Gysbert van Tonder said.

'Don't need them,' came from Chris Welman by way of endorsement.

'When you're there you just know it,' Gysbert van Tonder added. 'You can feel it in your bones.'

'Bones,' Chris Welman echoed, his voice sepulchral. It made you think of the mortal remains of some unhappy traveller lying bleaching in the sun.

'But where Meneer Vermaak is wrong,' Gysbert van Tonder said, 'is in thinking that when you are there you would want to go in further, after some passing Bushman or Bechuana has told you that it's the Forbidden Country. Because that's sure to happen. At some time or other a Bushman or Bechuana is sure to come up to you to ask for tobacco. And then you are also certain to ask him which is the best way of getting to where you want to go. Because it doesn't matter if you're going by a map, and you've got a very good map. Or if the way got explained to you so clearly at the Indian store in Ramoutsa that you just can't miss it.

'For, by the time the Bushman comes up to you to ask for tobacco, you are sure to have already passed a whole line of koppies that it says nothing about on the map. You will already have come across three dry river-beds and a deep donga and a petrified forest that not a word was spoken of in the instructions you got in the Indian store at Ramoutsa. I mean, it's always like that with a road you can't miss. After the first half-hour you know you should have had more sense than to have listened to the Indian. It is also not nice for you to know that you will one day be held accountable for all the things you have thought of the man who made the map.

'So you're glad when you come across that Bushman. Or, if it's a Bechuana, you're just as glad.'

Chris Welman interposed to say that the only time you were not glad was when it was a Mshangaan mine-boy, and he was riding a bicycle on his way home from the mines, and he came and asked you where he was.

What you at least felt about that Bushman, Gysbert van Tonder continued, was that he was not the dishonest kind of person who would deliberately mislead a stranger. You couldn't think of him as working behind a store counter, for one thing. Nor could you think of that Bushman as sitting down with a ruler and a pen and ink and drawing a map that would get printed to confuse the unsuspecting traveller, Gysbert van Tonder said.

'And after you've told that Bushman where you want to go, he'll point to the right or the left,' Gysbert van Tonder continued, 'you must turn off for half a day's journey, he'll say, before you again go on. It's also not impossible that the Bushman will point straight back, along the way you've come, and he'll make it clear to you that it doesn't matter very much whether, after that, you remember if it's the right or the left, you've got to turn to – just as long as you don't waste any time about getting straight out of where you're in.

'You'll have guessed, by that time, that where you are in is in the Forbidden Country.

'The Bushman will also most likely advise you not to waste time in cutting off some roll-tobacco to hand him. Just drop the whole roll where you are, right in the sand, he'll say, and he'll pick it up himself afterwards. He doesn't mind how much sand there is on the roll of tobacco, the Bushman will tell you, just as long as you get out of the Forbidden Country in time.'

But he still didn't see why, the schoolmaster said, you had to turn back, simply on account of an ignorant Bechuana or a Bushman. No sensible person would be influenced by that sort of thing, young Vermaak said.

It wasn't the same thing, Gysbert van Tonder explained, as sitting in Jurie Steyn's post office, drinking coffee.

'It's quite different, when you're out there,' Gysbert van Tonder said. 'When you're in the Tsifulu. With nothing but the sun and the sand and the thorn-trees. You feel quite different about things there. And if somebody tells you, then, that that area is forbidden country, you just take one look at it, and you know that it is so. I mean, it's no good saying it here, where we're sitting, now. You've got to be there, actually in the Tsifulu, to understand it. It's – well, it's Africa, there, see?'

'Afri—' Chris Welman started to chime in, and then checked himself because it sounded foolish.

'But will anything happen to a person that goes into that part of the Tsifulu that's forbidden?' the schoolmaster asked.

'No, I don't think so,' Gysbert van Tonder said. 'Nothing more than would happen to him anywhere else, I suppose.'

'Well, would he come back alive, for instance?' young Vermaak enquired further.

Gysbert van Tonder looked surprised.

'Alive? I don't see why not,' he said. 'I mean, there's nobody going to murder him there, is there? What's there about it that he shouldn't come back alive?'

It was the schoolmaster's turn to look puzzled.

'I don't get it,' he said. 'If there's nothing going to happen to you for going into that part of the Tsifulu – just nothing at all – then what's going to stop you from going there?'

'Because it's Forbidden Country,' Gysbert van Tonder said.

'Forbidden,' Chris Welman said.

Thereupon the schoolmaster asked Gysbert van Tonder and Chris Welman if they would go into the Forbidden Country, the two of them going in together, if they were in that part of the Tsifulu – seeing that nothing would happen to them for it.

'The Lord forefend,' Gysbert van Tonder said, his voice sounding hollow.

'God *forbid*,' Chris Welman said.

That kind of talk seeming to be getting nobody anywhere, Oupa Bekker made mention of an excursion he had once made into the Forbidden Country in the very old days.

'I was young, then, of course,' Oupa Bekker said, by way of apology. 'And another thing was that in those days there was a Swiss mission station in the Forbidden Country. So I thought perhaps it would not be too bad to go in there, after all. I had a whole lot of glass beads on my wagon to trade with the natives for cattle. I don't know how that story got around that natives, who are cattlemen themselves, would be so foolish as to trade off a cow or an ox for glass beads. In any case, I never found any that would. And after a chief offered me some brass wire for two of my lead oxen I knew it was no use trying any more, either.

'I camped out for a quite a while near the Swiss mission station. And in the evenings I would go over and talk to the missionary. He was glad to see me because, since it was the Forbidden Country, there was no white person, with the exception of his wife and daughter, that he had to talk to from one year's end to the other.

'The missionary's daughter had quite a simple name – Ettie. And she had laughing eyes and dark hair. And she used to bring us in coffee while her father and I sat talking. One night when she came in she smiled at something I said. The next night when she gave me my coffee her hand brushed against mine. The night after that she was at the front gate, in the starlight. And that was the last time that I saw Ettie.

'It was on account of the missionary coming upon us unexpectedly, from behind, just as I was reaching sideways over the gate to kiss Ettie, that I didn't see her again, of course. Because he was a Swiss missionary, I don't think it meant very much to him about it's being starlight. And the next thing I learnt was that Ettie had been sent back to Switzerland for more education.

'I don't need to tell you that I felt very bad about it – and for a long time, too. Naturally, I knew that it was the Forbidden Country, there, right enough. But still I couldn't help feeling that it needn't have been quite as forbidden as all that.'

Ramoutsa Road

You'll see that grave by the side of the road as you go to Ramoutsa, Oom Schalk Lourens said.

It is under that clump of withaaks just before you get to the Protectorate border. The kafirs are afraid to pass that place at night.

I knew Hendrik Oberholzer well. He was a man of God and an ouderling in the Dutch Reformed Church.

Unlike most of the farmers who lived here in those days, Hendrik Oberholzer was never caught smuggling cattle across the line. Perhaps it was because he was religious and wouldn't break the law.

Or else he chose only dark nights for the work. I don't know. I was rather good at bringing cattle over myself, and yet I was twice fined for it at Zeerust.

Hendrik Oberholzer lived on the farm Paradyskloof. When he first trekked in here he was already married and his son Paulus was about fourteen. Paulus was a lively youngster and full of spirits when there was drought in the land and there was no ploughing to be done.

But when it rained, and they had to sow mealies, Paulus would be sulky for days.

Once I went to Paradyskloof to borrow a sack of cement from Hendrik for a sheep-dip I was building. Paulus was in the lands, walking behind the plough.

I went up and spoke to him and told him about the cement for the sheep-dip. But he didn't stop the oxen or even turn his head to look at me.

'To hell with you and the cement,' he shouted. Then he added, when he got about fifteen yards away, 'and the sheep-dip.'

For some time after that Hendrik Oberholzer and I were not on speaking terms. Hendrik said that he was not going to allow other men to thrash his son.

But I had only flicked Paulus's bare leg with the sjambok. And that was after he had kicked me on the shin with his veldskoen because I had caught him by the wrist and told him that he wasn't to abuse a man old enough to be his father.

Anyway, I didn't get the cement.

Then, a few days before the minister came to hold the Nagmaal, Hendrik called at my house and said we must shake hands and forgive one another. As he was the ouderling, the predikant stayed with him for the three days, and if he was at enmity with anybody, Hendrik would not be allowed to take part in the Nagmaal.

I was pleased to have the quarrel settled. Hendrik Oberholzer was an upright man whom we all respected for his Christian ways, and he also regularly passed on to me the Pretoria newspapers after he had finished reading them himself.

Afterwards, as time went by, I could see that Hendrik was much worried on account of his son. Paulus was the only son of Hendrik and Lettie.

I knew that often Hendrik had sorrowed because the Lord had given him no more than one child, and yet this one had strange ways. Because of that, both Hendrik and his wife Lettie became saddened.

Paulus had had a good education. His father didn't take him out of school until he was in Standard IV. And for another thing he had been to Sunday School since he was seven.

Also his uncle, who was a builder, had taught Paulus to lay flat stones for stoeps. So, taken all round, Paulus had more than enough learning for a farmer.

But he was not content with that. He said he wanted to learn. Hendrik pointed out to him what had happened to Piet Slabberts. Piet Slabberts had gone to high school, and when he came back he didn't believe in God.

So nobody was surprised when, two months later, Piet Slabberts fell off an ox-wagon and was killed by the wheels going over his head.

But Paulus only laughed.

'That is not at all wonderful,' he said. 'If an ox-wagon goes over your head you always die, unless you've got a head like a Bushman. If Piet Slabberts didn't die, only then would I say it was wonderful.'

Yes, it was sinful of Paulus to talk like that when we could all see that in that happening was the hand of God.

At the funeral the ouderling who conducted the service also spoke about it, and Piet Slabbert's mother cried very much to think that the Lord had taken away her son because He was not satisfied with him.

Anyway, Paulus did less and less work on the farm. Even when the dam dried up, and for weeks they had to pump water for the cattle all day out of the borehole, Paulus just looked on and only helped when his father and the kafirs could not do any more.

And yet he was twenty and a strong, well-built young man. But there was something in him that was bad.

At first Hendrik Oberholzer had tried to make excuses for his son, saying that he was young and had still to learn wisdom, but later on he spoke no more about Paulus. Hendrik's wife Lettie also said nothing. But there was always sadness in her eyes.

For Paulus was her only child and he was not like other sons. He would often take a piece of paper and a pencil with him and go away in the bush and write verses all day. Of course Hendrik tore up those bits of paper whenever he found them in the house.

But that made no difference. Paulus just went on with his sinful, wordly things, even after the minister had spoken to him about it and told him that no good could come out of writing verses unless they were hymns.

But even then it was foolish. Because in the Dutch Reformed Hymn Book there were more hymns than what people could use.

Instead of starting to work for himself and finding some girl to whom he could get married, Paulus, as I have said, just loafed about. Yet he was not bad-looking, and there were many girls who would have favoured him if he looked at them first, and from them he could have chosen a woman for himself.

Only Paulus took no notice of girls and seemed shy in their company.

One afternoon I went over to Hendrik Oberholzer's farm to fetch over a black sow that I had bought from him. But Hendrik and Paulus had gone to Zeerust with a load of mealies, so that when I got to the house only Hendrik's wife Lettie was there.

I sat down and talked to her for a little while. By-and-by, after she had poured out the coffee, she started talking about Paulus. She was very grieved about him and I could see that she was not far off crying. Therefore I went and sat next to her on the riempies bank, and did my best to comfort her.

'Poor woman. Poor woman,' I said and patted her hand. But I couldn't comfort her much, because all the time I had to keep an eye on the door in case Hendrik came in suddenly.

Then Lettie showed me a few bits of paper that she had found under Paulus' pillow. It was the same kind of verses that he had been writing for a long time; all about mimosa trees and clouds and veld flowers and that sort of nonsense.

When I read those things I felt sorry that I didn't hit him harder with the sjambok that day he kicked me on the shin.

'He does not work even as much as a picannin,' Hendrik's wife Lettie said. 'All day he writes on these bits of paper. I can't understand what is wrong with him.'

'A man who writes things like that will come to no good,' I said to her, 'and I am sorry for you. It is not good the way Paulus is treating you.'

Immediately Lettie turned on me like one of those yellow-haired wild-cats, and told me I had no right to talk about her son.

She said I ought to be ashamed of myself and that, no matter what Paulus was like, he was always a much better man than any impudent Dopper who dared to talk about him. She said a lot of other things besides, and I was pleased when Hendrik returned.

But I saw then how much Lettie loved Paulus. Also, it shows you that you never know where you are with a woman.

Then one day Paulus went away. He just left home without saying a word to anybody.

Hendrik Oberholzer was very much troubled. He rode about to all the farms around here and asked if anyone had seen his son. He also went to Zeerust and told the police, but the police did not do much.

All they ever did was to get our people fined for bringing scraggy kafir cattle across the line. The sergeant at the station was a raw Hollander who listened to everything Hendrik said, and then at the end told Hendrik, after he had written something in a book, that perhaps what had happened was that Paulus had gone away.

Of course, Hendrik came to me, and I did what I could to help him. I went up to the Marico River right to where it flows into the Limpopo, and from there I came back along the Bechuanaland Protectorate border. Everywhere I inquired for Paulus.

I was many days away from the farm, but as there was not much work at the time of the year, with the rains not yet come, it did not matter.

I had hardly got back home when Hendrik called. From his lands he had seen me come through the poort and he had hastened over to see me.

We sat down in the voorkamer and filled our pipes.

'Well, Lourens,' Hendrik said, and his eyes were on the floor, 'did you hear anything about Paulus?'

It was early afternoon, with the sun shining in through the window, and in Hendrik's brown beard were white hairs that I had not noticed before.

I saw how Hendrik looked at the floor when he asked about his son. So I told him the truth, for I could see then that he already knew.

'The Lord will make all things right,' I said.

'Yes, God knows what is best,' Hendrik Oberholzer answered. 'I heard about . . . They told me yesterday.'

Hendrik could not bring himself to say that which we both knew about his son.

For, on my way back along the Bechuanaland border, I had come across Paulus. It was in some Mtosa huts outside Ramoutsa. There were about a dozen huts of red clay standing in a circle amongst the bushes.

In front of each hut a kafir lay stretched out in the sun with a blanket over him. All day long those kafirs lie there in the sun, smoking dagga and drinking beer.

Their wives and children sow the kafir-corn and the mealies and look after the cattle. And with no clothes on, but just a blanket over him, Paulus also lay amongst those kafirs.

I looked at him only once and turned away, without knowing whether he had seen me, because he was dagga-drunk. The blanket came up only to his waist, so that the rest of his body was naked and red with the sun. Next to him a kafir woman sat stringing white beads on a piece of copper wire.

That was what I told Hendrik Oberholzer.

'It would be much better if he was dead,' Hendrik said to me. 'To think that a son of mine should turn kafir.'

That was very terrible. Hendrik Oberholzer was right when he said it would be better if Paulus was dead.

I had known before of low-class *uitlanders* going to live in a kraal and marrying kafir women and spending the rest of their lives sleeping in the sun and drinking bujah. But that was the first time I had heard of that being done by a decent Boer son.

Shortly afterwards Hendrik left. He said no more about Paulus, except to let me know that he no longer had a son. After that I didn't speak about Paulus any more, either.

In a little while all the farmers in the Groot Marico knew what had happened, and they talked much of the shame that had come to Hendrik Oberholzer's family.

But Hendrik went on just the same as always, except that he looked a great deal older, on account of his shoulders beginning to stoop and his hair to turn white.

Things continued in that way for about six months. Or perhaps it was a little longer, I am not sure of the date, although I know that it was shortly after the second time that I had to pay £10 for cattle smuggling.

One morning I was in the lands talking to Hendrik about putting more wires on the fence, so that we wouldn't need herders for our sheep, when a young kafir on a donkey came up to us with a note.

He said that Baas Paulus had given him that note the night

before, and had told him to bring it over in the morning. He also told us that Baas Paulus was dead.

Hendrik read the note. Then he tore it up. I never got to learn what Paulus had written to him.

'Will you come with me, Lourens?' he asked.

I went with him. He got the kafirs to inspan the mule-cart, and also to put in a shovel and a pick-axe. All the way to the Mtosa huts Hendrik did not speak.

It was a fresh, pleasant morning in spring. The grass everywhere was long and green, and when we got to the higher ground, where the road twists round the kranz, there was still a light mist hanging over the trees.

The mules trotted steadily, so that it was a good while before midday when we reached the clump of withaaks that, with their tall, white trunks, stood high above the other thorn-trees.

Hendrik stopped the cart. He jumped off and threw the reins to the kafir in the back seat.

We left the road and followed one of the cow-paths through the bush. After we had gone a few yards we could see the red of the clay huts. But we also saw, on a branch overhanging the foot-path, a length of ox-riem, the end of which had been cut.

The ox-riem swayed in the wind, and at once, when I saw Hendrik Oberholzer's face, I knew what had happened. After writing the letter to his father Paulus had hanged himself on that branch and the kafirs had afterwards found him there and had cut him down.

We walked into the circle of huts. The kafirs lay on the ground under their blankets. But nobody lay in front of that hut where, on that last occasion, I had seen Paulus.

Only in front of the door that same kafir woman was sitting; still stringing white beads on to copper wire. She did not speak when we came up.

She just shifted away from the door to let us pass in, and as she moved aside I saw that she was with child.

Inside there was something under a blanket. We knew that it was Paulus. So he lay the day I saw him for the first time at the Mtosas, with the exception that now the blanket was over his head as well.

Only his bare toes stuck out underneath the blanket, and on them was red clay that seemed to be freshly dried. Apparently the kafirs had not found him hanging from the branch until the morning.

Between us we carried the body to the mule-cart.

Then for the first time Hendrik Oberholzer spoke.

'I will not have him back on my farm,' he said. 'Let him stay out here with the kafirs. Then he will be here later on, for his child by the kafir woman to come to him.'

But, although Hendrik's voice sounded bitter, there was also sadness in it.

So, by the side of the road to Ramoutsa, amongst the withaaks, we made a grave for Paulus Oberholzer. But the ground was hard.

Therefore it was not until late in the afternoon that we had dug a grave deep enough to bury him.

'I knew the Lord would make it right,' Hendrik said when we got into the mule-cart.

Notes

In the biography of Herman Charles Bosman, *Sunflower to the Sun*, events in his life are related to his literary production. By presenting the stories in this collection in chronological order, with the appropriate biographical notes, an opportunity is provided for the reader to follow the development of Bosman's career. The first and last stories are not in strict sequence, but create a suitable beginning and end to this collection.

On To Freedom

Placing *On to Freedom* as the first story in this collection is consistent with Bosman's quirky sense of humour. It was first published on 24 July 1937 in the *South African Opinion* under the editorship of Bernard Sachs. Bosman had then been living in London with his second wife Ella Manson for over three years and had reverted from his post-prison pen-name Herman Malan to H C Bosman.

The Night-dress

On 13 February 1931 'The Night-dress' was the second of Herman Bosman's Marico-inspired stories to be published in Stephen Black's *Sjambok* under the heading 'Life as Revealed by Fiction'. It appeared the same month as the first instalment of his second Schalk Lourens story 'The Rooinek' in the *Touleier.*

Francina Malherbe

'Francina Malherbe' was the first Schalk Lourens story to be published in a Bosman-Blignaut magazine other than their literary monthly, the *Touleier*. It appeared in May 1931 of their weekly critical paper *The New LSD* under the heading 'Life as Revealed by Fiction' appropriated from Stephen Black's defunct *Sjambok* and ran concurrently with 'The Gramophone' (in the *Touleier*)

Karel Flysman

'Karel Flysman', an Oom Schalk Lourens story, was published in June 1931 in the only issue ever to appear of the *African Magazine* (formerly the *Touleier*). Commercially unviable, the *Touleier* was further inhibited by Bosman's abortive departure for London. (He got as far as Cape Town before turning back.)

'Karel Flysman' was Bosman's first experiment with the socio-political 'hensopper' theme to which he would return several times, developing and polishing it to the excellence of 'Mafeking Road', the title story of Bosman's first published collection. 'Karel Flysman' bore no signature at all.

Visitors to Platrand

'Visitors to Platrand', a Schalk Lourens story, was first published on 1 November 1935 in the *South African Opinion*, under the editorship of Bernard Sachs. Bosman had been living in London with his second wife Ella Manson since early 1934. He had gone to join John Webb, an expatriate South African colleague of the *Touleier* days, who was to help launch his career as a Fleet Street journalist. To fit his new image he abandoned his post-prison pen-name Herman Malan and signed his work H.C. Bosman.

Although they did produce a newspaper, *The Sunday Critic* (from January to October 1936), aside from one exceptional piece – a review of T.S. Eliot's *Murder in the Cathedral* – his contribution was uninspired in comparison to the pieces he was sending back to the *South African Opinion*.

Bushveld Romance

'Bushveld Romance', another Schalk Lourens story, appeared on 17 April 1937 in the *South African Opinion* under the editorship of Bernard Sachs. From his pen in exile Bosman contributed verse, essays and such well-loved stories as 'Veld Maiden', 'In the Withaak's Shade', 'The Music Maker', 'Willem Prinsloo's Peach Brandy', and others, many of which formed the basis of his first collection of short stories, *Mafeking Road*.

Bosman's London period seems not so much to have provided him with the stimulus of a fresh environment, as to have confirmed his attachment to his old one.

Concertinas and Confetti

After Herman Bosman's return from England at the outbreak of World War II sheer poverty made him seek employment in areas both related and unrelated to writing. He actually worked on a building site at the bottom end of Twist Street before 1943, when a colleague recommended him for the post of editor of Pietersburg's bi-weekly United Party orientated newspaper *The Zoutpansberg Review and Mining Journal*. Then in March 1944 Leon Feldberg, founder editor of *The Jewish Times*, resuscitated the *South African Opinion* with Bernard Sachs as editor and Herman Bosman as literary editor. 'Concertinas and Confetti' appeared in the April issue.

Bosman had recently divorced his second wife Ella Manson on March 6, and, two weeks before the inception of the new *South African Opinion*, married Helena Stegmann, a school teacher he had met in Pietersburg. Through Helena he overcame a bad case of writer's block and even began writing poetry again; but his attachment to Ella persisted until after her death in April the following year. Strangely, the idea of lost love haunted him in real life, as it did in literature, and was a recurring theme to which he would return many times in stories like 'Concertinas and Confetti'.

The Story of Hester van Wyk

When Leon Feldberg revived the *South African Opinion* with Herman Bosman as literary editor it was privileged to have among its contributors Sarah Gertrude Millin, Nadine Gordimer, Doris Lessing, Alan Paton, Uys Krige, Nicholas Monsarrat, Gordon Vorster and Lionel Abrahams. Bosman contributed short stories, essays, literary and art criticism and reprinted some of his earlier poetry, saving 'work in progress' for reasons best known to himself. He also personally pounded the pavements to sell enough advertising space to help keep it going. 'The Story of Hester van Wyk' appeared in its fourth issue.

Camp-fires at Nagmaal

By June 1945 when 'Camp-fires at Nagmaal' appeared, the *South African Opinion* of the forties had been going for fifteen months; and Bosman's second wife Ella Manson, whom he could never abandon permanently, had been dead for three. Although 'Camp-fires at Nagmaal' proceeds gently at the pace of the ox, there appeared, also in the *Opinion* in the June and July issues two essays on cities and dorps respectively. They were motifs that preoccupied his first novel *Jacaranda in the Night*. In the same issue as 'Camp-fires at Nagmaal' he wrote: 'The difference between the city and the farm is, alas, age-old. The city has gutters.'

Treasure Trove

The February issue 1947 had been Bosman's last as literary editor of the *South African Opinion*. By mid-year he'd published his first novel *Jacaranda in the Night*, translated the *Rubaiyat of Omar Kayyam* into Afrikaans for the Afrikaanse Kulturele Leserskring and accepted a position as their Cape Town representative.

It was a misconceived publishing venture; but by the time Bosman returned to Johannesburg in the winter of 1947 Leon Feldberg had amalgamated the *South African Opinion* with *Trek*. However he undertook to re-employ Bosman on a regular but modified basis. When Bosman's first collection of short stories *Mafeking Road* was published late in 1947 it was dedicated to Leon Feldberg. 'Treasure Trove' appeared in the October issue of *Trek* 1948.

The Recognising Blues

Using Bosman's reference to Cape Town and the typewriter on which the manuscript was typed as dating devices, 'The Recognising Blues' must have been written after his brief unhappy period as the Cape Town representative of the Afrikaanse Kulturele Leserskring in the winter of 1947.

I first encountered the story in the holdings of the Humanities Research Center at Austin, Texas, where the Bosman papers are presently lodged. In 1961, while on a lecture tour from the University of Texas, Professor Joseph Jones evinced an interest in Bosman and successfully negotiated for the acquisition of his papers on their behalf. Helena Lake, Bosman's widow and copyright-holder and Lionel Abrahams, his unofficial literary executor, agreed to this arrangement only after an appeal through the media failed to yield a local equivalent institution to undertake the responsibility of their preservation. To ensure their safety they were sent to Texas in batches, the last parcel being posted in 1962.

Great Uncle Joris

When 'Great Uncle Joris' appeared in the December 1948 issue of *Trek*, although Bosman was also contributing in Afrikaans to *Ruiter* and *Brandwag*, his magazine output was slender. He had poured his creative energy instead into *Cold Stone Jug*, that autobiographical novel he referred to as 'A chronicle: being the unimpassioned record of a somewhat lengthy sojourn in prison.'

The Ferreira Millions

In the latter part of 1949 Bosman changed his lifestyle radically. He left *Trek* and became a proof-reader on the *Sunday Express* by day, conserving his creative energy to write another novel at night. After abandoning two attempts on the subject of city life he began the first draft of his second novel on dorp life *Willemsdorp*.

In October 1949 Bosman began contributing to *The Forum* magazine; and on 1 April 'The Ferreira Millions' was the penultimate Oom Schalk Lourens story to appear in it. A fortnight later he began his Voorkamer series, of which he turned out one a week until his death on 14 October 1951. These later formed the basis for two collections in hard cover.

Although in many respects 'The Ferreira Millions' resembles 'Treasure Trove' (in *Trek* October 1948), these stories were written at least eighteen months apart: and one must accept that it was part of Bosman's style to return to a theme several times and experiment with different ways of telling it.

The Missionary

'The Missionary' appeared in the Janaury 1951 issue of *Spotlight* magazine followed by *The Traitor's Wife* in February. The Voorkamer series in *The Forum* was already nine months old; but far from considering the Schalk Lourens tales written out, *Spotlight*'s editor Brian Lello believed these two stories to be an auspicious start to a whole new *Spotlight* series.

He was not to know that the punishing schedule Bosman had set himself – proof-reading by day so that he could finish *Willemsdorp* by night, except for Thursdays when he wrote one *Forum* piece a week – left little time or strength for other priorities. These were stories (written or rewritten mostly in Afrikaans) for the bilingual magazine *On Parade*, his *Spotlight* material and an anthology of South African English verse for Afrikaanse Pers Boekhandel, on which he and Gordon Vorster had collaborated but were never to complete.

'The Missionary' explores the same motif as *Graven Image*, published in English in *On Parade* after Bosman's death.

Rosser

'Rosser', which returns to the same theme as 'The Gramophone' (in *Mafeking Road*) and *Old Transvaal Story* (in *Unto Dust*) is the only story of this collection drawn from Bosman's Pretoria Central Prison experience on which he based his autobiographical novel *Cold Stone Jug*.

'Rosser' appeared seven years after Bosman's death in the 1958 spring issue of *The Purple Renoster*, edited by Bosman's pupil, disciple and unofficial literary executor Lionel Abrahams, who was responsible for the publication of six books drawn from his works. During the dozen or so issues of *The Purple Renoster* (1957–72) Herman Bosman posthumously kept company with writers like Barney Simon, Ahmed Essop, Ruth Miller, Oswald Mtshali, Wally Serote and Ezekiel Mphalele. I think he would have liked that.

The Murderess

'The Murderess' was the first of a series of Bosman stories to appear in the magazine *Personality* eighteen years after Bosman's death. They were brought to the attention of the editor Robin Short by Victor Mackeson, producer of the first of Patrick Mynhardt's one-man shows drawn from the works of H C Bosman.

The reference to corundum mining, dates 'The Murderess' after Bosman's period as editor of the *Zoutpansberg Review and Mining Journal* in 1943. But the juxtaposition of bushveld motifs against city ones that preoccupied much of Bosman's last novel *Willemsdorp* suggests that it was written during the last years of his life.

The Question

'The Question' is the second in the *Personality* series published eighteen years after Bosman's death. Although the narrator is not identified by his traditional '(Oom Schalk Lourens said)' label, his style is reminiscent of the way Schalk Lourens would have told it.

The Red Coat

'The Red Coat', an Oom Schalk Lourens story, was among the Bosman papers lodged at the Humanities Research Centre, Austin, Texas. A 'hensopper' story, as was Karel Flysman (1931), Bosman's reference to the decline of malaria in the Waterberg district is a clue that this story was probably written after the discovery of DDT when Dr Siegfried Annecke made dramatic strides in bringing malaria under control after World War II. It was probably one of the last Schalk Lourens stories Bosman wrote.

From 'In die Voorkamer'

In April 1950 Bosman started writing his 'Voorkamer' series of bushveld sketches for *The Forum* at the rate of one a week. Format apart, there are some marked differences between the 'Oom Schalk Lourens' stories and the 'Voorkamer' sketches. Whereas the former encompass the entire Marico landscape, the latter are mostly fragments of conversation in Jurie Steyn's 'voorkamer', where the people of the district gathered to await the arrival of the mail. This difference in setting is brought out subtly but convincingly. Without any specific descriptive passage in either series, one is immediately aware that with Oom Schalk Lourens one is outside where the horizons are wide, and in the later series one is inside where the walls are for leaning against. Even the dust smells and tastes different.

The 'Voorkamer' series is also set in another age. Progress had come to the Marico since the days of Oom Schalk and his frontiermen, when the main preoccupation was survival and the preservation of the chosen way of life. Vital issues had become casual reminiscences. The main occupation now seemed to be 'geselskap', something in which Bosman himself must have participated during his stay in the Marico in 1926.

Further differences that occur to one are compounded by the distinctive characteristics of the humour of each. The runaway switchback sense of exaggeration coupled with the casual throw-away line of the 'Schalk Lourens' stories as opposed to the low-keyed, mildly funny observations with the occasional 'non-ending' type of ending in the 'Voorkamer' series.

Ramoutsa Road

'Ramoutsa Road' appeared under Bosman's post-prison pen-name Herman Malan in the Bosman-Blignaut critical weekly the *New LSD* on 16 May 1931 – the same month as his other Schalk Lourens story The Gramophone appeared in the *Touleier*. Written much earlier than most of the pieces, 'Ramoutsa Road' provides a fitting climax to this selection.
of the pieces.